Blood is Thicker

By

Orlando A. Sanchez

A Montague & Strong Detective Agency Novel

"The blood of the covenant is thicker than the water of the womb."
-Unknown

ONE

A BITING WIND cut across the water as we landed on North Brother Island. We stepped off the ferry and onto the slick, deserted dock. The dawn rain pelted my face until Monty gestured and formed a shield around us, stopping the cold droplets from landing.

Peaches, fearing I might be too dry, shook the water off his body, drenching me, but somehow missing Monty.

"Really? Thank you," I groaned, shaking off the water. "It's not like I was soaked or anything."

<*This water is cold and I don't like being wet.*>

"You need to lay off the pastrami. Then you would have less surface area," I said, looking down at him as we walked. He appeared to be a Cane Corso, but was really the offspring of Cerberus, minus the mythological two heads. He stepped close to me and kept pace, as we walked off the dock and onto a short boardwalk. The boards creaked under our weight as he padded by my side.

<Are you saying I'm getting fat?>

"There's no *getting* about it. You sound like you're going to break through the boardwalk. Maybe Ezra has a low-fat pastrami option."

<Low–fat? Those words are sacrilege. Pastrami and all related meats are essential for my wellbeing and the safety of humankind. Speaking of which, are we going to eat soon?>

"I told you to stay home, but you wanted to come." I ignored his nudge into my leg. "We'll swing by Ezra's on the way back—you can eat then."

He responded with a low rumble as we kept walking.

"Are you talking to your creature again? You need to find a less overt method of communication." Monty looked at me. "One that doesn't make you appear as insane as you are."

"Everyone talks to their dogs," I said, patting Peaches on the head. "It's even therapeutic and healing."

"Everyone talks *to* their dogs not *with*, and that" — he glanced at Peaches—"barely qualifies as part of the *dog species*," Monty said while peering farther inland. He narrowed his eyes, pointing with the small wooden box he was holding. "That way."

"I didn't even know these islands existed," I said, pulling my coat tighter against the elements. Monty seemed unaffected by the cold. "Are you sure he's here? She could have lied. Dragons aren't known for their honesty."

"We checked the South Island and his energy is in the vicinity. Check the device again."

The Hack, after recovering from nearly losing Manhattan to a black hole, had finally answered my calls. I assured him the city wasn't going to disappear in some cataclysm, and he'd grudgingly provided me with his latest 'magical tech.'

He called it a runic filter. It looked like a smartphone, but thicker. According to the Hack, it was designed to detect spikes in magical energy and could distinguish between ambient and magical energy in any environment. When I pressed the screen, three blips showed up on the topographical map of the island.

"Monty, I think we have a problem," I said, and showed him the screen. "Which one of those is your brother?"

"The dragon lied," he said with a smile. He examined the filter closer. "This is actually good news."

"Why am I not surprised?" I handed him the filter. "Do you think she even saw your brother or was it all smoke? And, excuse me, 'good news'?"

He nodded and pushed some hair out of his face. "I don't know the purpose of Slif's deceit. What I do know is that these mages are quite powerful," he said, closing his eyes. "They must have found a way to replicate William's energy signature."

"And this is good news because…?" I said, confused. "Wait, how do you know they're mages?"

"It's good news because there's a possibility William is still alive. And I know what they are because I can sense them irrespective of this device" —he held up the runic filter—"and it seems we're here to have a conversation."

"Shit, can we just go back the way we came and avoid this *conversation*?" I said, shaking my head. "They never end well, mostly because they're heavy on the fireballs and light on the actual conversing."

"How did they mimic William's energy signature?" he said, rubbing his chin and handing me back the filter. "They must possess something of his with a recent imprint. It's the only way they could have recreated a signature so powerful."

We arrived at the only standing structure on the island. It was a hospital erected at the turn of the nineteenth century to deal with a smallpox outbreak—but now long abandoned. The building was partially intact, but trees and undergrowth had reclaimed most of the property. In front of the hospital, a circle roughly fifty feet in diameter had been cleared away. Covered in runes, it held a small pulsing orb in the center.

"That looks recent," I said, pointing at the circle before looking around into the trees. I pressed the runic filter again, but it came up blank. "Looks like they left. Maybe they got tired of waiting for you?"

"Unlikely," he said, narrowing his eyes as he surveyed the area. "I still sense them. They must be close."

Three figures materialized inside the cleared circle. They wore black robes with deep hoods that covered their faces. Each of the robes was trimmed in gold brocade. A large golden circle was embroidered on the chest of each.

Peaches dropped into a 'pounce and maim' posture and rumbled next to me. He lowered his head and spread his forepaws, the muscles of his back rippling with anticipation.

"Golden Circle police?" I asked as I opened my

jacket to give me easier access to my weapons. "The 'dark and ominous' thing works well for them."

"Envoys—messengers sent to escort rogue mages back to the Sanctuary," Monty said, and shook out one hand. "Usually by force."

The Envoy in the center stepped forward and pushed back his hood. A look of recognition crossed Monty's face. The Envoy appeared to be in his mid-thirties, with long blond hair tied back in a ponytail. He gave me a cursory glance and let his dark eyes settle on Monty, with a look of disappointment.

"Friend of yours?" I asked, taking a step back and letting my hand rest on Grim Whisper. "I get the impression he doesn't like what he sees."

"Gideon, I see you've been made an Envoy," Monty said with a nod. "When I left, you were still an apprentice. How are you?"

"Better than you," Gideon answered and formed an orb of fire in his hand. The two Envoys next to him did the same.

"Why do mages always default to fireballs?" I whispered under my breath, drawing Grim Whisper. "They don't seem in the *conversing* mood, Monty."

Monty took a step forward. Gideon extended his other hand and formed a second fireball. "Don't do this, Gideon," Monty said, flexing his hands.

"Mage Tristan Montague, by order of the Tribunal of the Golden Circle, you are hereby instructed to surrender yourself to the custody of the Envoys," Gideon said, the orbs he'd formed floating lazily in front of him. "You will be returned to the Sanctuary to await judgment for the crime of casting a forbidden spell—a void vortex—in a populated area."

"And if I refuse?" Monty asked, keeping his eyes on Gideon, as he placed the small box he'd been carrying on the ground.

"Then we are authorized to use deadly force to carry out our mandate," Gideon whispered and moved into a defensive stance. "Don't make me hurt you, Tristan."

TWO

GIDEON DROPPED HIS hands and the orbs raced at Monty. I leaped to the side, expecting to see Monty next to me. I turned back and saw him standing where I'd left him.

"Impending orbs of flame?" I said, getting to my feet some distance away. "Isn't this the part where you jump out of the way?"

"No. This is the part where I do this" —he extended a hand palm up in front of his body, caught both orbs, and merged them—"and return them to their owner," he said with a slight grunt.

The merged orb crashed into Gideon and knocked him to the other side of the circle. The other two Envoys absorbed their orbs and rushed to his aid. Gideon got to his feet, shrugging off the hands of the Envoys who assisted him.

"He looks pissed, Monty," I whispered, looking at the approaching Gideon. "I thought you told me it wasn't wise to piss off a mage?"

"I said it wasn't wise for *you* to piss off a mage," Monty replied with a look. "I do it often. Their arrogance makes them easy to prod."

Gideon stood at the edge of the circle and stared at Monty. He took a breath to compose himself. I could tell he had a few choice words he wanted to use, but to his credit, he kept himself in check. Maybe he knew it was a bad idea to piss off a mage like Monty.

"You've shifted," Gideon said after getting his breathing and temper under control. "We were not informed of this change."

"I just informed you," Monty said matter-of-factly. "Go back to the Sanctuary before someone gets hurt, or worse."

"We weren't informed, but I came prepared just in case," Gideon said, reaching into his robe.

"Gideon—?" Monty said before Gideon pulled out what could only be described as a micro Uzi.

"What the hell?" I said as I pressed the main bead on the mala bracelet that Karma had given me. When I pressed the main bead, it usually created a large shield that protected me from damage. I say *usually* because it's been known to malfunction at times—but this time it worked.

I jumped in front of Monty and Peaches, grabbing Peaches' by his neck as he growled, and made sure he didn't jump into a hail of bullets. "Since when do mages use Uzis?"

"The Envoys are trained to adapt and overcome." Monty traced runes in the air as a hail of bullets pounded into the shield. "This is actually a sound strategy when facing a stronger opponent."

"I'm so glad you approve of his strategy." I held the shield up and braced my arm with my free hand. It felt like a jackhammer on my forearm. "Can we apply a strategy of our own? One that stops the bullets from turning my arm to jelly would be good."

"I've been wondering about the shield-generation of the mala. If it's kinetic, this should keep the shield up indefinitely. My theory is that it transforms kinetic energy—in this case the energy of the rounds—into the repulsive energy of the shield," he said, releasing the runes into the air. "This will be a good test to see how long your shield lasts."

"Really, this? You consider *this* a good test?" I said, aware of the bullets trying to turn us into Swiss cheese. "You think we could try a less lethal method of testing?"

The bullets stopped. I peered over the shield to see Gideon getting another magazine. Monty gestured with his hand, and the other two Envoys were suddenly yanked from the circle. They were slammed into a nearby wall with incredible force and then they crumpled to the ground. Monty stepped forward with another gesture, and the Uzi fell to pieces in Gideon's hands. It reminded me of my recently disintegrated, tailor-made Armani suit jacket he'd decided to test that spell on.

"You unbound it?" Gideon said as he dropped the pieces of the Uzi and pulled out a blade. His voice was laced with fear and awe. "Have you gone dark, Tristan?"

"Bollocks! What's this bloody obsession with my going dark?" Monty said as he closed on Gideon. "You only ask because you've never met a dark mage. If I were a dark mage, you and your team would be bloody smears inside this circle."

Gideon lunged forward, and Monty jumped back.

"I think it's a fair question, considering the void vortices you unleashed *inside* a city," Gideon said, slashing horizontally. "You cast a spell that could've killed everyone—a forbidden spell."

"There were...*extenuating circumstances*," Monty said, stepping inside the arc of the slash, grabbing Gideon's wrist, and twisting, stripping him of the weapon and slamming him into the ground. "A dragon was trying to cook us."

"Be that as it may," Gideon said in between gasps as he lay on his back, "the law is clear."

"This is why I left the Sanctuary," Monty said, holding the blade to Gideon's throat. "Go back and tell them to leave me alone. I shut down the vortex and the city wasn't destroyed. How did you find me, anyway?"

Gideon scoffed. "Find you? We never lost you. The Elders allowed you to think you were on your own. You're an *Ordaurum*—they will never leave you alone."

"How did you get William's signature? Where is he?"

"Only the Elders know that." Gideon squirmed away from the blade pressing into his neck and drawing blood. "I was given that"—he pointed at the center of the circle—"and told to bring you home."

Monty stood up and moved to the center of the circle. He took the small orb and put it in a pocket. "You go back and tell them I'm already home," Monty whispered with quiet menace as he stepped out of the circle. "If I see you again, I won't be so pleasant."

The other two Envoys stumbled back to Gideon's side. That's when I recognized it. They were standing in a large teleportation circle. Gideon stood up, rubbing his neck where Monty had held the blade to it.

"You may have defeated me, but they will send an Arbiter. I will inform them of your shifted status. You won't defeat the Arbiter," Gideon said and touched the center of the circle. A moment later, it flared a blinding white light and they disappeared. Monty waved a hand at the circle and the concrete crumbled, destroying it.

Monty fell to one knee and gasped for breath. I stepped over to him and he waved me off as he got unsteadily to his feet.

"You okay?" I asked, concerned, and extended a hand, which he took. "You're looking a little paler than usual."

"I'm not accustomed to the cost of using elevated magic. I need to eat, meditate, and get some rest." Monty walked back to the box he had placed on the ground. "Let's do this and get back."

I nodded. "Can you stop an Arbiter?" I asked, stepping back and out of the way as he traced a rune over the ground. "How powerful are they?"

"I don't know," he said after a pause. "Arbiters are to mages what MPs are to the military. They police the mages, which means they are the most powerful among us. When sent on a recovery, they are judge, jury, and executioner."

"Maybe the Elders will just forget about you?" I looked down as the box holding the runed platinum and Davros' essence sank into the ground and disappeared.

"No. Gideon was right. They will never leave an *Ordaurum* alone. I'm too important to them. They will send an Arbiter. If I don't return, he will try to destroy me."

"That's some retirement plan." I looked out over the water to the incoming ferry. "If the Elders know where your brother is, then it may be—"

"It may be time to visit the Sanctuary," Monty said.

"Isn't that what they want, though? Except maybe with you in restraints?"

"Exactly." He pushed some hair out of his face. "I'll go back on my terms, not theirs. We need to go see Erik for that."

"The Hellfire Club?" I gave a short cough to clear my throat. "Erik doesn't exactly want to see me these days."

"What did you do?" Monty said slowly as he turned to look at me. "Is the club still intact?"

"Excuse me? You're the one who does magical demolitions, and it isn't even my fault—Quan walked through the place and set off all his defenses because she was pissed at *you*."

"He must have been livid," Monty said with a small smile as he rubbed his chin. "Did he ban you?"

"More or less. He told me not to come back unless invited," I replied. "But I'm sure you could convince him."

"We'll give him a day. Right now, I need to get home. Let's do Roselli's tonight. I'm famished." We stepped on the ferry and floated away from the island.

"Do you think he'll let me bring Peaches again after last time?" I asked, rubbing Peaches' head. "I'm sure he could behave."

<I promise not to bite anyone who doesn't deserve it.>

"After his last visit and the disaster that ensued?" Monty said, shuddering as he looked down at Peaches, who did his best to look unassuming and gentle but failed epically as he bared his teeth. Monty shook his head. "I've seen worse at Roselli's. I'll make the reservation."

THREE

THE SUN HAD set a few hours earlier by the time we got back to the Moscow. Andrei was by the door as usual as we got out of the Goat. The engine of the 1967 Pontiac GTO purred and rumbled as the valet took it down to the garage.

"*Dobryy vecher,*" Andrei said, holding the door open as we entered the building.

"Good evening, Andrei," I said, walking past him. "Where's Olga?"

He stepped back when Peaches came through the door behind me.

"*Tseber, bozhe khrani menya,*" Andrei said under his breath, crossing himself as Peaches entered the lobby, oblivious to the terror he left in his wake. I walked back to the door and Andrei.

"He doesn't understand Russian yet," I whispered as I put a hand on his shoulder. "If you keep calling him a hellhound, I'm going to teach him, and then not even God will save you when he decides to remove one of your legs. His name is Peaches. *Vy ponimayete?*"

"*Da*," he said, nodding quickly. "I understand. Mrs. Olga is not in building. Will be back later."

"*Spasibo*," I said, and caught up to Monty and Peaches as they reached the stairs. "Tell her I have this month and next, but we need to talk about my neighbors."

"Your creature is going to give him a heart attack one day, and you will have to explain to Olga why her doorman is dead in the lobby," Monty said as we approached our door.

He placed his hand on the sign next to our space, and it flared orange, releasing the locks to the door. I looked at the sign again. We had to have the last one replaced due to Monty not getting the runes quite right and melting the brass. But this one wasn't quite right.

"Why is my name second again?" I asked, polishing a corner of the sign. "It sounds better with Strong first —Strong & Montague Detectives or S&M Detectives."

Monty sighed as he opened the door. "*This* again? I explained it to you. The names are arranged alphabetically," he said and pointed at the sign. "It's also a matter of professionalism. We are a detective agency, not a BDSM outlet."

"Can we increase the size of my name—you know, to compensate and create balance?" I closed the door behind me. Orange runes flared along its surface, locking it.

"Balance?" Monty asked, giving me a look and heading to the kitchen.

"Size matters. You can't both be first *and* have a bigger font," I said, rubbing Peaches behind the ears.

"That's just not fair."

"Are you serious?" He poked his head out of the kitchen. "It's not the length of your name but the size of the font that matters?"

I nodded. "Exactly. When are we getting the new sign?"

"If it will put this subject to rest, I'll order it as soon as I have some tea—"

Peaches barked, cutting him off.

Standing under an F-22 Raptor as it broke Mach 1 would be quieter than Peaches' bark. The sound shattered the kitchen windows and nearly destroyed my eardrums. Someone or something had breached the external security and was coming our way.

I shook my head until the ringing calmed down and I got to my feet. I stepped around Peaches, who had planted himself in the center of the floor. Monty formed an orb of air in his hand as he approached.

I unholstered Grim Whisper and approached the door, when a blast of air shoved me out of the way. I managed to get my hand up to prevent an instant face-plant into the wall. I turned in time to see the door explode inward and sail across our reception area, missing the immobile Peaches by inches.

That's when I saw her. My heart clenched in my chest. I tried to process the image I was seeing, but the disconnect was too great and my brain seized.

She was slumped against the doorframe. Her face was bruised and bloodied. Her hair, normally perfectly arranged, was a mane of chaos around her head and face. The black leggings she wore were torn in several places, allowing glimpses of her pale skin. A bloodied hand clutched her abdomen.

"I need—I need help. *Cazadoras*," she said, struggling with the words.

Her breathing was ragged as she grasped the doorframe and left a bloody trail. The runes on the threshold flared to life as she stumbled forward. Peaches rumbled but stood still. She took a few steps forward as she tried to regain some measure of composure and failed. Her body crumpled to the floor a second later.

I stared down in shock at the unconscious form of Michiko the leader of the Dark Council, and the most powerful vampire I knew.

"Are you just going to leave her on the floor?" Monty said, exasperated. "I'll get something to clean all this blood. Call Roxanne."

"You know you could've just yelled at me to get out of the way. An air blast into the nearest wall seems a little much." I crouched next to Michiko and scooped her up gently, walking over to the sofa.

"No time," he said from the kitchen. "Besides, you seem unhurt. And don't put your bloody vampire on the Hansen."

I froze mid-descent. That's *exactly* where I was about to place her. The Hansen sofa had been a gift from Roxanne, and it was *the* most expensive item in our reception area. No one was allowed to sit on it, except Roxanne on her infrequent visits.

"She's not my bloody vampire" —I looked down at her in my arms—"well, today I guess she is."

"Precisely, and I don't intend to get blood all over that thing. Roxanne will kill me and attempt to kill you if we get it soiled."

"How about the Chesterfield? Or do you have a gurney around here somewhere that I don't know about?" I said, looking around. I stepped over to the other sofa and laid Chi down.

"Chesterfield, yes." Monty appeared with a bunch of towels and a small steel box covered in runes. "Step back. Did you call Roxanne?"

"On it." I pulled out my phone, dialed Haven Medical, and put it on speakerphone.

"Haven Medical. Director DeMarco speaking," Roxanne said after she picked up. "Hello, Simon."

"Roxanne, we have an emergency," I said, my voice urgent. "You need to come to the office."

"Simon, every time I deal with you or Monty it's an emergency," she said with a sigh. "Is it Tristan? Bring him here. You aren't equipped to deal with injuries at your office."

"No, we can't transport," I said. "I think she's lost too much blood."

"She? What happened?" she said, suddenly alert. "Who's injured?"

"It's Chi. You need to get here now."

"Shite, I'm on my way. Tell Tristan to keep her stable until I arrive. I'll be there in twenty minutes."

"She knows I'm not a bloody healer," Monty grumbled as he placed towels around Chi and attempted to clean her wounds. "You'd better cancel Roselli's."

"Cancel…Roselli's?" I looked at my phone. "And speak to Piero?"

He gave me the 'are you an idiot?' look and I began

dialing. "Would you like to explain to your vampire how you felt obligated to go to dinner while she lies on the sofa, bleeding?"

"Not really, but cancelling Roselli's is almost as bad," I said, hoping Piero didn't pick up. His voice came over the phone after the third ring.

"Roselli's," his voice said with a slight accent. "Buona sera, Simon."

"Buona sera, Piero," I said and took a deep breath. "I'm afraid we can't make it tonight after all."

There was a long pause followed by a short sigh.

"This is unacceptable. I *needed* to speak with you and Tristano tonight," Piero said, in short clipped words, which meant he was upset. I could just see him tapping a finger into the table, punctuating each word. "You know the consequence of cancellation?"

I did. You didn't cancel a reservation at Roselli's—ever. The penalty for doing so was blacklisting for a year, if you were lucky and Piero was in a good mood.

"Someone attacked Michiko—" I started.

"Ah, Simon, why don't you speak clearly?" he replied. I imagined the face pinch. "I will bring you dinner."

I tried my best to hide my shock. Piero owned the most exclusive supernatural dining experience in the city. To offer to bring us dinner was unprecedented. After a few seconds, I found my voice.

"Piero, that is extremely gracious of you, but I'm sure you must be busy. The night is just starting and I can't possibly expect you to—" Monty gave me the 'don't bother' headshake. "Can you bring some pastrami for Peaches?"

"Pastrami?" Piero answered as if I had insulted him. "This is not a *deli*. I will bring filet for the animal, and he *will* eat it."

"Thank you, Piero, this really means—" I began.

"I will be there *presto. Ciao*," he said, cutting me off and hanging up.

"He must *really* like you," Monty said, exchanging towels and applying bandages. "I don't recall him delivering food to anyone in my lifetime. Much less their pet."

"I think it has less to do with me and more to do with *her*." I pointed at Chi. "She is the head of the Dark Council, after all. How is she? What could do this to her? Why isn't she reacting?"

Chi was deathly still and paler than usual.

"It's a defensive state. Stronger vampires can enter a catatonic state to deal with catastrophic injury," Monty said, tossing down a towel and picking up a new one.

"How strong is she? She has a gunshot wound and is checked out. This 'defensive state' seems like it needs to be reworked," I said, looking down at her.

"With a younger or less powerful vampire, you would be sweeping up the remains," he said and glanced up at me. "I don't know how she survived a gunshot to the abdomen, but whoever did this is obviously dangerous and skilled."

"Who can do that? As far as I know there aren't many things as fast as a vampire."

"The staggering breadth of your supernatural knowledge leaves much to be desired. There are creatures as fast as— and faster than—vampires in existence," he said, shaking his head and pushing some hair from his face. "But this was done by the *Cazadoras*, or so she claims. I just don't remember them using guns."

"The wound isn't closing. I thought vampires had accelerated healing?" I said, concerned that the pile of bloody towels on the floor was growing. When she woke up, she would be starving. We would be standing next to a powerful, old, and hungry vampire. "Monty, what happens when she wakes up?"

"Well, she usually heals almost as fast as you do, but she's still losing blood from her abdominal wound." Monty placed more blood-soaked towels on the floor. "When she wakes up she will be ravenous, and will need to feed—oh. That would be bad."

I nodded and checked Grim Whisper. I didn't want to shoot her, but I had no plans of being on the menu. "Yes, that was my thought too. Will restraints work?"

"No, she's too strong. Even in this state, her body would resist them. If *Cazadoras* did this, they were trying to kill her," he said, his voice grim. "I thought the *Cazadoras* were wiped out? Seems I was mistaken."

"What are these *Cazadoras*?" I lifted the door and placed the hernia-inducing piece of metal next to the entrance with a grunt. "Remind me again why we have a door if it keeps getting blown off its hinges? Maybe we should just hang a curtain?"

"Their full name is *Cazadoras Sangrientas de la Noche*— Blood Hunters of the Night," Monty answered, ignoring my remark about the door. "They've always been referred to as Blood Hunters."

"And, what, they're vampire hunters?" I said with a short-lived laugh as Monty nodded. "They're *really* vampire hunters?"

"Precisely. They were the most effective, zealous, and ruthless group to hunt down vampires. I thought the Council declared New York a sanctuary city?" he said, looking concerned at Chi.

"Seems someone didn't get the memo," I said. "Could be they just don't care about the Council and really hate vampires—or both."

He placed a bandage over the wound and kept towels over it, applying pressure. "Whatever caused this wound is still in there. I don't dare go in without knowing what I'm looking for."

"Can't you just use your magic? Quan did this thing with golden light that healed me and Peaches. Can you do that?"

"I'm a battle mage not a healer. My specialty is destruction, not reconstruction." Monty gave me a look of uncertainty. "Besides, magic on supernaturals is far from an exact thing. I could do more harm than good."

"Yeah, I got the part about destruction, so did most of the city." I removed the bloody towels from his side. "Don't they teach you to fix what you break back at the Sanctuary? Isn't that one of the tenets?"

"Battle mages are taught to be living weapons of obliteration," he said tightly, and sighed. "What Quan did is a discipline beyond me. The mages of the White Phoenix are unparalleled healers. I can only do rudimentary healing spells," he whispered. "All we can do now is wait."

FOUR

ROXANNE APPEARED AT the door a few minutes later with a large case and two assistants carrying a gurney. Peaches let Roxanne cross the threshold but growled when the men tried to come in. They both stopped at the threshold and stepped back.

<Can I bite them? The large one looks crunchy and we never went to the place to get meat.>

"Piero is bringing over food." I grabbed Peaches by the scruff of the neck and pulled him away from the doorway. "Sorry, he likes to chew on visitors."

"Please, wait by the entrance," Roxanne instructed her assistants while she put her case down and knelt on the floor next to Monty. She touched his wrist with her hand. "I can take over from here. Thank you, Tristan. Would you mind assisting?"

He gave her a short nod, moved to the side, and opened the case. She put on a pair of latex gloves and asked for a scalpel.

"Some of the wounds around the neck and torso

have healed." Monty handed her the scalpel. "The abdominal injury must contain some foreign material that's preventing healing."

"Do you know who did this?" she asked as she made the first incision. "Who could bring her down like this?"

"Blood Hunters," Monty said, and dabbed the wound with absorbent material to remove the blood.

"Blood Hunters? I thought the Council eliminated that group decades ago," Roxanne said, reaching for the angled forceps. "This is a gunshot wound. Since when do Blood Hunters use guns? I thought they were all crossbows and stakes?"

"Apparently they've upgraded with the times. Can you remove the round? I would like to examine it before you report it to the NYTF," Monty said, wiping more blood away.

Like any medical facility, Haven Medical was obligated by law to report every case of a bullet wound, gunshot wound, or any other injury from a firearm. Instead of reporting to the local police, they had to inform the NYTF—a quasi-military police force created to deal with any supernatural event occurring in New York City.

Roxanne nodded and closed her eyes for a few seconds. She traced a rune and the tip of the forceps turned white hot before returning to its normal color. She grabbed another forceps, uttered some words under her breath, and inserted them into the wound.

After what seemed like a minute, she removed the instrument with the round and placed it into the small pan he held. She inserted the first pair of forceps into the wound, and the sound of sizzling skin filled the reception area as she cauterized the wound.

Monty stood up and stepped over to a table as Roxanne dressed the wound. He motioned for me to come over as he pulled out a magnifying glass from one of the drawers. He wiped down the round, removing blood, and exposing an intricate inscription of runic symbols.

"Do you know what this is?" he asked me as I looked at the round.

It appeared to glow as he turned it in his fingers. "Is that thing glowing?" I asked as he kept rotating the bullet.

He nodded. "Yes. This is a nine-millimeter armor-piercing light irradiated tungsten carbide round—the ultimate vampire killer," he said, the surprise evident in his voice. "LIT rounds were outlawed after the war. These things are impossible to get."

"Not that impossible. Looks like your entropy rounds, with a slight variation." I pointed at the bullet. "I don't recognize the rune work, though."

"I don't either, but I know who would," Monty whispered, turning the bullet over in his hand under the magnifying glass. "Nicholas."

"Are you kidding me? Nicholas, as in the Moving Market? Shadow Nick?"

"The same," he confirmed, nodding while he examined the bullet. "Rune designs are like signatures. Each one is a distinct indicator of who traced it. He would know who created this rune."

"And probably tell them, too. We can't trust him." I tried to memorize the design.

"You don't trust him because he's a plane-weaver," Monty said, looking at me.

"Am I wrong?"

"Yes," Monty said. "We can't trust Nicholas because he's a corrupt, immoral, and self-serving individual who will betray you faster than you could blink."

"How am I wrong, then? That's exactly what I meant—you can't trust him."

"It has nothing to do with his being a plane-weaver," Monty said, examining the bullet again. "It has everything to do with him being a despicable person. You have to respect his ability. The Moving Market thrives and eludes the Dark Council because of him. He's a necessary evil."

"Are you sure he's the only one who can identify these runes? Does this mean this design is like handwriting?" I asked, clearly not happy about this Moving Market idea.

"Deeper. A rune possesses a miniscule essence of the magic-user who wrote it. If he doesn't know who wrote it, he will know someone who does." Monty held up the bullet and looked at Roxanne. "I need to borrow this for a few hours. Can you delay the call?"

"I'll call Ramirez once we get back to Haven," Roxanne answered and began packing her case. "That should give you a few hours' head start. You can take the bullet, but we need to take her with us, she's still critical. Simon, can you carry her to the gurney?"

I slipped my arms under the still unconscious Chi, and lifted her slowly off the Chesterfield. She was surprisingly heavy despite her small frame. Being careful not to jostle her, I placed her gently on the waiting gurney. I stepped back as they strapped her in and waited for Roxanne.

"Can you keep her safe? I need you to keep her safe," I said as Roxanne approached the gurney.

"The Unit is runed inside and out," she responded, placing her hand on my arm. "She'll be safe. I'll ride in the back with her. I may not be Tristan, but I'm no pushover."

"Thank you. I'll be there as soon as I can," I said, touching the side of the gurney. "I'll make sure to call Ken."

"That would be a good idea," Roxanne said, nodding and looking at our doorway. "Maybe a more secure door would be in order as well. This one seems to be a bit—*flimsy*. Don't you have Cecil's number, Tristan?"

"I do," he said, stepping close to her. "I'll give him a call."

"I'm sure he could design something for you." She motioned to the assistants and they wheeled Chi down the hall. She paused to touch Monty's cheek. "It's good of you to keep the Hansen clean. I need that bullet in Haven by the time the NYTF comes to speak to me."

Tristan turned crimson and nodded. She smiled and caught up to the gurney. Peaches and I followed her downstairs and to the waiting Unit. Once they were on their way, I came back upstairs in time to see Monty raising the door and placing it over the entrance.

FIVE

I CALLED KEN and it went straight to voicemail. This meant he was either busy, or avoiding me. He and I didn't get along much, but when it came to his sister, he was fierce—and scary—in his loyalty.

I had just fastened the last hinge on the door, when I heard a soft knock. Peaches sniffed the air and rumbled. I patted him on the head and rubbed his ears.

"Settle down, at least this threat has the courtesy to knock before exploding the door in my face," I said, stepping back and resting my hand on Grim Whisper.

"Simon, the door," Piero said, followed by another knock. I knew it was Piero because he always pronounced my name "see-mon" instead of the usual "sigh-mon."

"One second." I grabbed Peaches by the scruff. "I need to put you on a diet." He resisted my pull and focused on the door. Even I could smell the food.

<I smell meat. Delicious meat.>

"This food will go to waste if cold," Piero said in his

clipped English. *"Aprire la porta—presto, presto."*

I quickly opened the door and Piero entered without incident—or anything in his hands. Peaches expressed his disappointment as a low rumble escaped him.

Piero was dressed in a simple black Armani two-piece suit, and a bone-white shirt. As usual, his ensemble lacked any kind of neckwear. I had shared the bond with Piero shortly after taking Peaches to Roselli's a few weeks ago. Taking a hellhound to an upscale supernatural restaurant wasn't the best of ideas, and could be the reason he was making a house call.

Piero stood by the entrance and clapped twice.

A young woman came to the door. Her hands were trembling slightly as she held a large steel bowl. Inside the bowl, I counted no less than five oversized pieces of filet mignon. The smell wafted over, and Peaches looked at me and whined.

"You can't bite the brave young woman who is bringing you the meat," I said, making sure I had a firm grip on his scruff. "Got it?"

He rumbled in response.

<*I will focus on the meat. If you let me go, I promise not to bite her. Or anyone else bringing meat.*>

"Please, place the bowl over there. The kitchen," Piero instructed. "Away from the door. Thank you."

The young woman did as he asked, never taking her eyes off Peaches.

"Only the bowl," I warned as I let him go. He ran over with a singular focus, and began devouring the food.

The young woman backed out of the office quickly, as Piero clapped again. A cadre of white-clad servers

Blood Is Thicker

entered the office next. They rolled in a serving table and an assortment of trays. They quickly placed a setting for two on the Kahiko dining table, which elicited a nod of approval from Piero as he pointed and coordinated.

Ten minutes later the servers were gone, and we sat down before a magnificent dinner. Wagyu beef and white truffle covered my plate, and Monty had his signature salad. Piero stood by the table. If I closed my eyes and went by smell alone, I could almost imagine we were in Roselli's.

"Who did you leave at Roselli's?" I asked, grabbing my utensils. "Who's running the shift tonight?"

Piero waved my questions away. "Roselli's is where I am. Tonight"—he waved his hand around with flair—"*this* is Roselli's," he said.

"Piero, you said you needed to speak with us," Monty said as he began to eat. "When are you leaving?"

"Tonight," Piero said after a brief pause. "After this meal, Roselli's will be closed until I return."

"Leaving? Why are you leaving? And where?" I said around a bite of the wagyu that melted in my mouth and made me pause. "This is incredible."

Piero nodded sagely. "Some old enemies have come to the city. I will leave to keep my people and my business safe. We will go somewhere safe."

I made the connection. "You're talking about the Blood Hunters. Why would they be after you?" I asked, looking at Monty as he reached in his pocket.

"*Non capisco*," Piero said. "This city is *campo neutro*. We don't attack and we are left alone. This has changed."

Monty placed the LIT round on the table, and Piero narrowed his eyes at it. "Do you recognize this ammunition?" Monty asked.

Piero flexed his jaw as he nodded slowly. "Those are the bullets of the ones who kill my kind—*cacciatori di sangue*," he said, his voice thick with emotion. "Blood Hunters. This is why I came to speak to you. When you told me about the attack on the *Concilio Negro*, I knew they were here."

"You knew they were coming?" I said.

"Rumors, whispers in the night, but nothing certain," he said with a short nod. "Many of the old ones didn't believe me. 'The Blood Hunters are gone,' they said. 'You worry for nothing. *Cacciatori* are a myth, ghosts from a different time. They are all dead.'"

"Looks like they aren't *all* dead," I said, looking at the round on the table. "One of these Blood Hunters tried to kill Michiko."

"They are not all gone," Piero whispered, and shook his head. "The *Cacciatori* are looking for something. Something powerful enough to risk a challenge to the *Concilio Negro*, but I do not know what."

"We need to go see Nicholas," Monty said as he grabbed the round.

SIX

PIERO SAID HIS goodbyes and left after we ate. He confirmed that if we wanted to find out who made the LIT round, the black market was the best place to look.

Every community has a dark side—the face that's kept hidden from outsiders and revealed only at night when you're reckless, desperate, or both. It's the face of dark alleys, whispered promises, and cold steel inserted slowly between your ribs as your life spills out into the street.

The magical community was no exception. The only difference was that this black market dealt in unchecked lust, lethality, and magic. If you needed a spell to fry an enemy on the spot, or some runes to make yourself irresistible, you could find it in the Moving Market.

The hard part was finding the Moving Market itself.

Nicholas Casimir ran the Moving Market. Everyone knew him as Shadow Nick because he was a plane-weaver. As a mage, he was probably-low to mid-level in power. As a plane-weaver, he was off-the-charts incredible. His ability allowed him to displace an entire city block and move it in the interstices, the spaces in-between moments of reality.

Monty said it was similar to what I did with my mark, but on a scale that would melt my brain if he tried to explain it to me. The Moving Market was never in one place for too long. You had to find it by going to where it was going to be and entering a space it would occupy. After ten minutes, the entrance would disappear again.

We grabbed our gear and headed downstairs. Peaches padded silently next to me. Andrei saw us coming and backed away from the door while muttering something I couldn't catch. Olga towered behind the reception desk.

Olga Gabriella Rodensky Etrechenko was the reason the term 'ice queen' was invented. She looked down at me with her imperial gaze and gave me a brief nod, barely acknowledging my existence. She wore a dress that screamed 'obscenely expensive' and that highlighted the curves of her statuesque figure. Monty kept walking and stepped outside to wait for the Goat.

"Stronk, you want to speak to me?" she said, never able to manage the 'g' at the end of my name. "What is wrong with neighbor?"

"We need more space for the office and I never see them open. Can you ask them if they would be willing to give us more floor space?" I asked, looking into her glacial blue eyes. "We're willing to pay the increase in rent, obviously."

She shook her head slowly. "They are very important

lawyer firm, and your detective agency"—she wobbled her hand palm-down, indicating instability—" is *slabyy*, very shaky," she replied while looking at Peaches, who returned the gaze unflinchingly. "That is hellhound Andrei speaks of?"

"Yes. His name is Peaches and he's a good dog. Not a hellhound." I gave Andrei a sidelong glance. I reached into my coat pocket to remove an envelope, and placed it on the desk in front of her. "This month and the next two. I would appreciate it if you could ask them."

No one cheated Olga and survived long enough to talk about it. I wasn't certain about what she was, but I knew she wasn't entirely human.

"*Persiki*," she said, still looking at Peaches and taking the envelope from the desk. She nodded and broke eye contact with him, looking up to stare at me. "He is good dog, Stronk, special. I will ask the lawyers if they give you more space."

"Thank you, Olga." I headed to the entrance and slowed my pace as we drew near the door, just to give Andrei an extra second or two next to Peaches. I was considerate that way. Monty was outside standing next to the Goat. "Why don't you ever speak to her?"

"Because I have grown rather fond of our offices and would prefer to avoid not leveling the building," he said as I grabbed the door handle and the surface of the Goat flared orange. The engine unlocked to hammer on anvil sounds as we got inside and I started the car. The engine roared and settled into a thrumming purr as Monty closed his eyes and made a gesture. Runes came to life inside the car.

"What do you mean 'not leveling the building'? Not

that I *want* you to level the building."

"There is only one way a prolonged conversation between your landlady and I can end," Monty said with a sigh. "Which is why we don't speak. Now, do you want me to go speak to her and unleash havoc, or do we go find the Moving Market?"

"I prefer the non-havoc option," I said, throwing the car in gear. "Where to?"

"The Highline near the Hudson Yards," he said, opening his eyes. "The market should be there in an hour, which gives us plenty of time."

An orange moon raced behind us as we sped up the Westside Highway to meet Shadow Nick and his Moving Market.

SEVEN

IF MASTER YAT had one saying, it would be—*"The blow you don't see coming hurts the most."*

This was followed with a few whacks of his stick, which lit up every pain receptor in my body.

"See, you didn't expect that, and so the pain is exquisite, isn't it?"

"That's one way to describe it," I said, gasping for breath.

A few more strikes, too fast to detect or prepare for, introduced me to deeper levels of agony.

"Smartass remarks will bring you new and much deserved pain. Run the drill again."

These words rushed back to me as the Westside Highway suddenly went from flat road to ramp beneath us.

"This…is not good," I said. The world tilted as we launched into the air, barrel-rolling. In the distance, I managed to glimpse a figure off to the right, but it was too far away to get any details. Whoever had attacked us had opted for targeting the road and not the car.

"Monty—a little help?"

Behind us, I could hear Peaches rumble his displeasure.

Monty gestured as we turned. The Goat righted itself and descended, cutting the arc of the jump short. We landed hard enough to bounce once and slide several feet.

"I don't want to get on that ride again," I said as I shook my head. In the distance, I saw the figure, dressed in the dark, hooded robe with a large golden circle on the chest. "Your Envoy buddy doesn't know when to quit."

I drew Grim Whisper and took aim.

"Don't shoot him—yet," Monty said as the figure approached. "He may listen to reason."

I pointed to the asphalt ramp we'd just Evel Knieveled. "Reason? I have a few reasons he can listen to, while I shoot his ass for launching me into space." I put one bullet in the chamber.

Monty looked at me. "Let me speak with him. I've known him since he was a boy."

I lowered Grim Whisper, and Peaches rumbled in the back. "Go ahead." I waved him forward. "He so much as moves a finger to pick his nose, that big gold circle on his chest becomes target practice."

<*Can I bite the man hiding his face?*>

"Monty wants to try and reason with the mage who just tried to kill us, boy," I said, rubbing Peaches' head. "Let them talk it out, but be ready to shred Tall, Dark, and Spooky."

<*I'm ready. I'm also hungry. Can we go to* the place?>

"No, you need to lay off the pastrami. Didn't you

just eat filet? Where did that go? I swear you have a black hole instead of a stomach."

We got out of the car. Monty walked several feet away and stopped. He pulled on the sleeves of his jacket, as the robed figure closed the distance.

"You think your shift makes you immune to the mandate of the elders?" Gideon asked, pushing the hood back. "You think you're untouchable, beyond reproach? I know your history. You're—"

"…Getting aggravated," Monty said, extending an arm to the side. "You need to go home, Gideon."

Gideon formed two orbs of flame in his hands. I glanced to the side, but it looked like Gideon was riding solo on this mission. That was a mistake. At least with his friends around to distract Monty, it would take a few moments before he got to pounding on Gideon. All alone meant he had all of Monty's attention.

"Listen to what he's telling you and go home," I yelled from where I stood, next to the Goat. Monty held up a hand and I shut up. I stepped to the other side of the car just in case some debris or a young mage flew my way.

"You don't get to tell me what to do," Gideon answered, releasing the orbs. They floated in front of him, bobbing slowly in the night. "You're not even a mage—you're some kind of freak."

"Ouch, no need for insults," I said, raising Grim Whisper. "You don't see me saying anything about you wandering my city in your oversized dressing gown with a big golden target on your chest." Peaches shifted into 'pounce and maim' mode.

"Gideon, it's time for you to leave," Monty

whispered into the night as he stepped closer to him. "I would rather it be without pain, but we are quite pressed for time."

"Pressed for time? Pressed for time!" Gideon yelled, and brought forth several more orbs of fire. "I'm so sorry to inconvenience you, oh battle mage Montague. Allow me to send you promptly to your death!"

Gideon thrust both hands forward, unleashing the group of orbs at Monty. I kept my hand near the main bead on my mala, in case one of the orbs veered off course and decided to pay me a visit. "Monty?" I said, stepping behind him. "That's a buttloa—bunch of orbs coming your way. You got this?"

"Of course, but you may want to step back," he said as he traced a rune in the air before him. Blue trails followed his fingers as they moved through the air. I took several steps back. The racing orbs streaked through the darkness and then slowed down, stopping a few feet away from Monty.

Clearly, this didn't impress Gideon, who reached in his robe and pulled out a shotgun. I saw the surfaces of the barrels were covered with nasty, angry-looking runes.

"Those runes don't look pleasant, Monty. What kind of Mary Poppins pockets does that robe have?" I asked, moving back. "Tell me it isn't one of those 'time and relative dimensions in space' things you mages love to carry."

"This would be a good time to shoot," Monty said, waving his hand forward and reversing the orbs back at Gideon and moving back with me. "Try not to get shot by those rounds."

Gideon slid to the right and shot at the orbs. A latticework of white energy erupted in front of them. It surrounded and dissolved the orbs before disappearing. I fired at the large golden circle on his chest. It was dark and I was moving, so I missed my shots.

"When I said shoot, I meant *at* him," Monty said, waving a hand and forming a pair of shields around him. "Or were those warning shots?"

"It's not easy hitting a moving target while running at night, on uneven terrain, and taking fire," I said indignantly. "It's not as easy as I make it look."

I managed to slide across the hood of the Goat, just as another one of those lattice rounds slammed into the car. Peaches ran at Gideon, and blinked out on the way there.

"Gideon, stop this while you still can," Monty said, forming another shield. "Acting alone to apprehend a rogue mage is an unsanctioned act for an Envoy. I'd hate to see you demoted back to apprentice."

"You always were an arrogant bastard, Tristan. I'm going to enjoy humiliating you," Gideon said, tossing the shotgun to one side. He waved both arms up and then swung them down. The street behind Monty rose like a wave. It crested above him close to thirty feet high, and came crashing down as Monty pressed his hands together.

The shields around Monty slammed together, sandwiching him. At the same time, Peaches reappeared in front of Gideon mid-pounce.

The asphalt wave crashed around Monty, leaving him unharmed and without a speck of dust on his suit. He made a grabbing motion with his hands, and formed two spheres of asphalt the size of bowling balls, which he launched at Gideon.

Peaches tucked his head and dog-pedoed Gideon, before disappearing again. Gideon tried to dodge the canine battering ram and failed. He took the hit in his abdomen and doubled over. As the spheres flew toward him, he lifted his arms, covering his body.

The two asphalt bowling balls barreled through his block. He screamed in pain as the bones of his forearms shattered with an audible snap.

Monty approached Gideon, who was now hunched over and groaning. He crouched down to look at Gideon's arms, gently talking hold of each one.

"I warned you," Monty said. "Pointing out the error of your current course of action is hardly a demonstration of arrogance." Gideon's screams echoed into the night as Monty tightened his grip on the broken limbs. "The radius and ulna are fractured in both arms, and need medical attention. Are you ready to go home now?"

<*Can I bite him now? His arms are bending the wrong way. Can I take them off?*>

"Leave his arms alone, boy," I whispered, rubbing Peaches behind the ears as he rumbled contentedly. "You did good."

"I will stop you, Tristan," Gideon gasped through clenched teeth, tears of pain streaming down his face. "I'm an Envoy, and I will bring you to justice."

"Gideon," Monty said softly, "maybe one day you will stop me, but that day is not today. Haven or the Sanctuary?"

"The Sanctuary. I will not be treated and placed in a cell by your *dark sorceress*," Gideon said, spitting out the last words. "Yet another reason to bring you in. You defile yourself with the dark arts, *mage*."

I held my breath in anticipation of the incineration of Gideon—clueless Envoy of the Golden Circle, who met his demise by opening his mouth one time too many and insulting someone with enough power to erase him. It was a major error in judgment. I should know: it was a neighborhood I visited often.

Monty's jaw flexed, and for a second I thought he really was going to blast the helpless idiot on the floor who had just had both his arms snapped like chopsticks. Instead of a searing fireball, though, Monty smiled and nodded.

"You're right, Gideon. I am defiled. If you ever slander any of the people I care about again, I promise you I won't be so courteous. Do you understand?" Monty grabbed one of Gideon's forearms and squeezed. More screams. "I'm going to take that as a yes."

Gideon nodded mutely as Monty gestured and formed a large rune under him.

"Monty, isn't that a teleportation circle?" I asked, as Gideon's eyes opened wide and he started shaking his head.

"Very observant, Simon. It *is* a teleportation circle. How else do you propose I get him back to the Sanctuary—carry him?" Monty said, looking at me and pointing at Gideon.

"Just saying, those things have some nasty after effects," I said, looking down at Gideon. "The ones at

Hellfire twisted my intestines and gut-punched me, and I only traveled a short distance. I heard that the effect is based on how far it sends you."

Monty gave me a very slow smile and nodded. "The effect of intra-abdominal pressure and discomfort you experienced is a direct correlation to the distance traversed through magical deconstruction and reconstruction—or teleportation, as you call it." He turned to Gideon and gestured. "This is going to hurt quite a bit. I hope you had a light dinner."

"No, wait, don't—" Gideon said, as Monty touched the circle. Gideon convulsed for a few seconds and disappeared.

"You didn't have to go all magicsciencey on me. A simple yes would've worked." I looked at the fading circle. "Is he going to survive that trip?"

"It will feel like his intestines are being ripped out—with a dull butter knife, but he will survive." Monty headed to the Goat. "We don't have all night, so let's go."

"Have I told you how scary you are?" I opened the back door and let Peaches into the car. I slid into my seat, as he rocked the suspension while settling into his backseat sprawl.

"Repeatedly and in great detail," Monty said, pulling out the bullet again and examining it. "I'd say it's a bit hypocritical coming from a time-stopping immortal who's bonded to a hellhound that regularly winks in and out of existence, trying to gnaw on whatever it can get its jaws on. But who am I to judge?"

"My point exactly," I said as we sped uptown. "You're definitely scarier than that."

EIGHT

"HOW DO YOU do it…remember them all?" I asked as we raced up the Westside Highway. "The gestures. How do you keep them straight? My fingers would be pretzeled if I had to do that all the time."

"The gestures are a physical manifestation of—"

"Oh no, more magicscience. Can you do this in plain English?" I groaned. "A description I don't need a degree in advanced quantum magical theory to understand?"

Monty sighed and rubbed his chin, then held up the bullet he was examining.

"You see this bullet?"

"No. I'm focusing on the road at the moment."

"It was a rhetorical question," he said. "The runes on this bullet are a physical manifestation designed to cause the most harm to vampires. When I trace a rune in the air, it's not only a physical act, but a measure of my will placed in the act."

"This is why you can trace the runes back to who

inscribed them?" I asked, giving him a quick glance. "But how do you keep them all straight? You must know hundreds of runes. I heard the wizard in Chicago has a wikiskull. It holds all of the hard-to-remember knowledge—and it talks."

"A *wikiskull*—typical for a wizard. Most of them are slightly unhinged, after all," Monty said with an air of disdain. "The last wizard I spoke to—what was his name?—Mincemeat or Rindwince? In any case, he was completely round the twist."

"I'm going to guess that means mentally unwell?" I said, swerving around traffic and keeping an eye out for any more Envoys.

"He kept going on about how he discovered some ancient tome that described the world as a large disc, sitting on the back of four elephants, which in turn stood on the back of a giant turtle."

"What? Really? He thought the Earth was flat?"

"Not flat—the world was a disc, according to him. When I asked him for this supposed tome, do you know what his response was?"

"I don't know, but he sounds like a lot of fun," I said, trying not to burst into laughter. Monty took his mageness very seriously. "What did he say?"

"He said the librarian has it."

"That makes sense. Old tome kind of goes with librarian."

"I proceeded to ask to speak to said librarian. He told me I needed to bring bananas because the librarian in question loves them," Monty said, putting the bullet in a pocket.

"Sounds like a healthy librarian," I said, smiling. "We

can all stand to eat better—in fact, I'm getting hungry."

<Are we going to eat soon?>

"No, you black hole. You just ate a little while ago," I said, shooting Peaches a glance in the rear-view mirror.

"Then he tells me the librarian is an orangutan," Monty said, deadpanned. "He is an actual *Pongo pygmaeus.*"

"Hey, I know you don't like wizards, but insults?" I said, giving him another look. "Wait, he's a real mon—?"

"Never use that word." Monty glanced at me sharply. "The correct term is *ape.*"

"Ape? *Really?*" I barely held it together.

Monty nodded and looked out his window. It took all of three seconds before I burst out laughing.

"This is why wizards and their ilk are unstable. All those years buried in books addles their brains—which is why they *need* wikiskulls," he said, making a gesture. "We have about fifteen minutes."

"So how do mages remember?" I said, stifling another laugh. "Don't you have a ton of things to remember and recall? What do you have? An elephant?"

"Droll," he said, reaching for a powerbar. "Mages have an elegant solution to recall. We use the 'method of loci' or mind palace."

"And that works?" I asked, incredulous. "You create little rooms and remember everything?"

"It's better than a talking skull since it can't be misplaced."

"Unless you lose your mind," I whispered as the Hudson Yards came into view. "Same entrance?"

Monty nodded as we left the car parked outside the station. I locked the Goat and Peaches nudged my leg. We walked into the newest addition of the MTA's 7 line. I gripped the handrail as we stepped onto the escalator. The steepness of the angle made me feel like I was going to fall forward at any moment. Monty looked at his watch, completely unperturbed. "Three minutes," he said as we stepped off the vertigo-inducing moving stairway.

We walked to the far side of the floor and headed to a maintenance door. The sign read "electrical closet." Several minutes later, a bright light flooded the doorframe. Monty grabbed the handle and opened the door. We entered a small foyer, where a man stood at the far end with his back turned to us.

"I still think this is a bad idea," I whispered as Monty closed the door behind us. "This guy is about as trustworthy as Peaches is with pastrami."

"Nicholas Casimir provides a necessary—if overpriced—service to the magic-user community," Monty whispered back. "He has a habit of stranding people 'in-between' planes. Don't anger him. Remember, we go wisely and slowly. Those who rush, stumble and fall."

"Did you just 'Bard' me?" I said, noticing Shadow Nick turning at the sound of my voice. He gave us a smile as he approached. "Head's up—something slimy this way comes."

NINE

"TRISTAN, *SIMON*, AND—companion," Nick said, looking at Peaches. He said my name with the same tone I used when my milk went bad—transforming to old, smelly, and chunky yogurt. I got that reaction often from magic-users. It's mostly because I'm immune to magic and they aren't immune to bullets. "Welcome to the Market. This is truly a pleasure. What kind of animal is that?"

"His name is Peaches," I said, placing a hand on Peaches' head.

"Of course it is," Nick answered with his shark smile. "He is quite wonderful. Are you here to sell him?"

Nicholas Casimir was unassuming. He had black hair, cut short in the back, long on the top and tied into a man-bun. It made him look like an urban samurai minus the swords—and any sense of honor. He stood about average height, and opted for dressing in what I called 'hipster casual'—jeans with a pair of brown oxfords, and a light gray dress shirt with the tails outside the pants. Piero would have a fit if he saw him, and would immediately try to fix the shirt while insulting his lack of fashion sense.

The look was intentional. He was an average mage, but an incredibly powerful plane-weaver. Plane-weavers could travel between planes with ease. It allowed them to go literally anywhere with a thought. Nick took this a step further and transported a city block with him.

"Peaches isn't for sale—*ever*," I said, resting my hand lightly on Grim Whisper. "Are we clear? Or is this going to be a problem?"

"Crystal," Nick said, the smile vanishing. "How can I expedite your visit?"

"Are you *rushing* us, Nick?" I looked around the foyer. "I was thinking we could visit some of the shops, maybe even have dinner."

We stood in Market Central. The entire market was arranged like a wheel formed of seven concentric circles. This building, which also doubled as Nick's base of operations, acted as the hub of the wheel. The rings were arranged in order of influence and power.

The higher ranked magic-users inhabited the rings closest to the hub. The two outer rings were a no-man's land. If you found yourself on an outer ring, it was only a matter of time before someone or something tried to relieve you of your ability to breathe. The only law in the market was the law of the jungle: only the strong or clever survived.

"*Rush* you? Never," Nick answered with feigned surprise, holding his hands up in surrender. "I just prefer my buildings intact and, well, you two have a reputation for demolition. Now, how can I help you?"

Monty reached into his pocket for the bullet, and I saw Nick tense up. His eyes darted behind us and to the right. Like I said, slimy as hell. I walked over to the wall and stood to the right of the entrance to the foyer. I put my back to the wall and my hand on Grim Whisper. Peaches sat on his haunches next to me, his eyes fixed on Nick.

<I don't like him. Can I bite him a little?>

"He probably tastes horrible," I whispered, bending over to rub his chest. "Keep your eyes on him though."

Peaches rumbled in response and moved to his relaxed 'pounce and shred' stance as I stood up.

Monty held the bullet up for Nick to see. A shadow crossed Nick's face, but he regained his composure immediately.

"I have need of your particular expertise, Nicholas," Monty said, handing Nick the bullet. "I need to know who runed this."

"I am humbled and honored to be of service," Nick replied with a short bow, looking at the bullet. I wanted to hand him a shovel since he was really piling it on. "I'm afraid I don't have an answer for you. I don't even know what kind of ammunition this is."

"He's lying, Monty," I said, and pushed off the wall. "You know exactly what kind of round that is."

"Nicholas, that is a LIT round," Monty said. "I'm not asking if you sold it. Because we both know you wouldn't truck in illegal, banned, and unsanctioned munitions that would bring several sects, mine included, knocking on your respectable door."

"Quite right," Nick said, giving me a stink-eye and

turning the bullet over in his fingers. "I'm respectable and wouldn't deal in such things."

"But," Monty said with an edge that made Nick step back, "that round was used in an attempted murder. If you don't provide me with a name, someone is going to assume you had something to do with that attack."

"Me? I don't deal with LIT rounds. Taking out Dark Council vamps is bad business for everyone," Nick said quickly, holding a hand up. Peaches rumbled and sprawled his forelegs ever so slightly.

Monty nodded and formed an orb of white flame in his hand. "Except—I never mentioned the Dark Council or vampires," Monty whispered as he released the orb and let it float next to him. "The name?"

"You won't find him," Nick said with a sigh. "He's on ring seven. I only know the name he goes by."

"And what name is that?" I asked, already dreading the trip to the outermost ring. "What do you call him?"

"*I* don't call him anything," Nick said defiantly. "His people gave him the name—they call him Wraith."

TEN

NICK ESCORTED US to the Ringrail Station—the main method of travel between the rings in the Market.

"They're automated," Nick said, pointing to the rail car. "Once you pass ring five, only a Station Master can retrieve them. Here, you'll need this."

He handed Monty a small piece of blue plastic the size of a credit card. It contained the Market logo, of seven concentric circles surrounding a stylized NC. It was a travel pass, authorizing us to travel outward.

"Will that get us to ring seven?" I asked, looking at the card. "What about the return trip?"

"It will give you access outward. If you can make it back to the ring-five station, it will provide you access," Nick said, adjusting his shirt. "The outer rings are dangerous, with the seventh being the worst. Be careful."

We stepped on the rail car, and it slowly rolled away from the station and down the tracks.

"Am I supposed to believe he's suddenly concerned

about our safety?" I looked down the tunnel. "Did you notice how he said, 'if we can make it back'? That means he doesn't plan on us making it back."

"More likely he will announce our arrival to this Wraith," Monty said, sitting on one of the benches that were bolted into the floor. "There is a good chance we may be ambushed en route."

"Glad you're looking at this optimistically," I muttered as I sat next to him and rested my hand on Grim Whisper.

Travel between the rings was managed through transportation passages. Similar to subway tunnels, but shorter, with automated open-air rail cars that could go from ring to ring. Each station between rings one through five required a stop at a checkpoint.

From ring five to six, the tunnel was sealed, with a large blast door that only opened with Nick's authorization and a travel pass. We had both. We rolled to a stop as Station Master Five approached. He wore a nametag that read "Grant" on the left side of his uniform. I saw the runes glowing faintly on the large blast door. Even though I couldn't read them, I had a basic idea of what they meant.

Once you pass this door, you're monumentally screwed. Enjoy what's left of your life—all thirty minutes of it.

When we indicated we were going outward, the Station Master only shook his head. "Your funeral," Grant said. "Don't try coming back this way. Once that door is closed, only Mr. Casimir can ask us to open it."

"We have his authorization," I said, pointing at the travel pass Monty held. "This says we can go outward and return."

"To go outward, yes—ring seven, if I understand correctly," Grant said, barely looking at the pass. "That's a one-way trip—in more ways than one."

He circled a finger around and over his head, and the station workers opened the blast door. We lurched forward as the rail car continued into the darkened tunnel. Monty formed an orb of light as we continued into the gloom. The tunnel was dark and empty, with Monty providing the only source of light.

<*I don't like this place and I'm hungry.*>

"Me either, boy. We'll get something to eat soon, promise," I said as we picked up speed.

We rolled into Station Six a few minutes later. Monty gestured and the orb vanished. There was a distinct difference between Station Five and Station Six. There was no Station Master to greet us. Papers and trash covered parts of the platform. The walls were dingy and gray, and some of the light fixtures were broken. I noticed there was no blast door between Station Six and Seven. The rail car came to a stop in the center of the platform. A display on the railcar began counting down five minutes.

"You know this is a trap, right?" I said, rubbing Peaches' head as we waited. I looked forward into the darkness of the next tunnel. "There probably is no Wraith, and Nick will try and kill you and banish me. Or vice-versa."

"Most likely the latter," Monty said with a nod. "He probably knows of your immunity to magic."

"Do we even know where to find this Wraith? It's not like this place is small," I said as the railcar lurched forward into another dark tunnel. Monty produced another light orb, and I could see this tunnel was in a greater state of disrepair than the one joining Station Five to Six. A few minutes later, we approached Station Seven.

"Somehow I don't think that's going to be much of a problem," Monty said as we entered the station. "It seems we are expected."

He let go of the orb, and it floated high above us into the vaulted ceiling. I looked at the station and realized we had a welcoming committee.

"What are those?" I said under my breath as we rolled to a stop. My nose tried to crawl off my face as the stench hit me. Even Peaches snuffled a few times as he rumbled in the direction of the group standing on the platform. It appeared to be a large group of homeless tunnel dwellers. Most of their clothing was tattered and dirty. Their faces were covered with strips of cloth, making it hard to see any clear features. "A little bit of disinfectant would work wonders down here. Do you have a disinfectant spell?"

"No, I don't," Monty whispered back as he narrowed his eyes at the group on the platform. "Some of these are accomplished mages. If you could manage not to anger them for at least three minutes—I would be grateful *and* surprised."

"Let me work my charm," I said, and Monty groaned. "I'll make sure to keep it civil and we can get this all sorted out. You should've seen how I handled Hel."

"Hel has a sense of humor—twisted as it is. I don't think these mages have any reason to laugh," Monty said, stepping off the railcar and onto the platform.

"Let me do the talking. At least that way when it goes awry I can see it coming."

"Don't you mean 'if it goes awry'?" I asked, standing next to him and opening my coat, making sure I had access to Ebonsoul.

"With us it's always a matter of when," Monty said as the group fanned out into a defensive semi-circular formation.

ELEVEN

I COUNTED SIX on the welcoming committee. Two unleashed fireballs, which raced at us. They may have appeared to be homeless, but they moved with the precision of a trained fighting force. Monty slashed the air, and a glowing blue shield materialized in front of us. It deflected the fireballs into a wall.

"I get the impression they don't want to talk." I drew Grim Whisper. "Maybe the Wraith is busy and this is his way of telling us to come back later?"

"Don't get too close to them, and keep him back," Monty said, pointing at Peaches. "They have magic dampeners around this station."

"Which means?" I asked, looking around for the dampeners, without a clue what they looked like. "You just made a shield. Your magic is fine."

"I should have been able to absorb those fireballs. That shield took entirely too much energy," Monty said, wiping sweat from his brow in between breaths. "It means—"

"Bullets and blades. My kind of conversation," I said, taking a step forward and reversing direction quickly as four of the tunnel dwellers whipped out guns of their own.

"Theirs too, it seems," Monty said as we backpedaled. "It looks like they have a larger vocabulary as well."

The rifles they held were large, mean-looking things, but it was hard to tell what they were carrying when we were busy jumping off the platform and onto the tracks, avoiding several more orbs followed by gunfire.

"What kind of rounds are you carrying?" Monty asked as he gestured. A fireball formed in his hand and fizzled out a second later. "Bollocks, the dampeners are increasing in strength."

With a grunt and a nod, he pulled out two narrow cylinders about six inches long. They were covered in runes that glowed blue in the low light.

"Considering where we are, I'm loaded out to deal with magic-users. I have persuaders, hollow points, and one magazine of entropy rounds." I checked Grim Whisper. "No silver rounds, though."

Persuader rounds were designed to scramble neural networks. They were ideal for dealing with magic-users and normals alike. They hurt like hell but were non-lethal.

When a round hit you, it caused your synapses to misfire all over the place. For mages, it meant no more spell-casting for a good ten minutes. It also made the target lose control of all bodily functions, and gave new meaning to the term "pissed-off mage." Probably another reason the magic community disliked me.

Monty looked at me as if I had gone insane. "Were you expecting a war?" He flicked his wrists, causing the cylinders to extend into thin batons that crackled with energy.

"I told you this was a trap," I said, making sure I had one round in the chamber. "When I see Nick, I'm going to introduce my boot to his nuts."

Monty nodded at my words. "I'll take the mages, you handle the rest. Don't kill them," he said, and peeked over the platform. He ducked down quickly when gunfire erupted above us. Peaches growled next to me and entered 'pounce and shred' mode.

<*I can bite a few of them, if I move fast.*>

"No, boy, you have to stay here," I said, grabbing Peaches rapidly by the scruff of the neck. "You won't be able to do your usual 'blink out and bash' move down here. They have runes in place to stop magic. Stay here."

I didn't know how he did his disappearing thing, but I figured it was magic-based. I didn't want to take a chance with the dampeners that he would blink out and not be able to come back. Or worse, not blink out at all and get shredded by their guns.

He rumbled in response but stayed close. I turned to Monty, who was fishing in his pocket for something.

"What do you mean don't kill them?" I adjusted the sheath holding the Ebonsoul. "What do you think they're trying to do with those bullets—give us a massage? What are you looking for?"

"This." Monty held up a small clear orb between two fingers. "A trap is only effective if you're unprepared for it."

"Monty," I said, with growing apprehension, "what is that?"

"This is—well, this is a gravity well," he whispered, with barely hidden admiration. From the tone, you would've thought I'd asked him about his favorite tea. "It's really quite effective and—"

"Again with the black hole?" I stared at him in disbelief. "Are you *trying* to kill us? Aren't you in enough trouble with the Golden Circle?"

"I said gravity well, not void vortex," he explained, holding the orb closer to me. "This will multiply the force of gravity by several orders of magnitude when it goes off. They will be forced to the floor due to their increased weight."

"What about the dampeners? Won't they stop it?"

"No. This enhances something that is currently present—gravity," he said, and gestured around the small orb. Several runes flared to life on its surface. "The same way magic doesn't affect you, but if I use the same magic to slam you with a lorry, it will do considerable damage."

"Thank you for that visual," I said, peeking over the platform edge to see a hooded figure emerge from the group. "Looks like the Wraith wants to talk, after all."

"Tristan, don't take this personally, it's just business," the hooded figure said. "I can't have you going around asking questions about those rounds. Word will get back to my clients, and I can't have that stain on my reputation."

"Wait a minute, that's—" I started.

"Nicholas, or should I call you Wraith?" Monty said, looking over the platform edge. "That was convincing theater earlier. I almost believed your act."

"You knew he was faking all along?" I asked as we climbed onto the platform. "Why didn't you scorch him back at Market Central?"

"Because he has information we need," Monty answered, taking a few steps to the side. "You did say one truth, Nicholas. *You* didn't make these rounds, but you do know who did. Do you want to tell me now, or later—after the pain?"

Nick laughed and motioned to his dwellers. They fanned out and shrugged off their outer layers. The ones holding the rifles were wearing hi-tech body armor. The two mages formed orbs of flame in their hands. Around their necks, I noticed glowing pendants to match the one worn by Nick.

"You have no power here, Tristan. The great Mage Montague will die on the dirty streets of the Market. Remembered by few and mourned by none," Nick said, forming his own orb of flame.

"Why not just attack us at Market Central? Why bring us out here? This is your place, after all," I asked him, resting my hand on Ebonsoul. This was going to go magey any second and I wanted to be ready.

"I needed to get you to the outer rings." Nick pulled back his hood. "Out here I can deal with the two of you without interference from the Council. On my rings I am judge, jury, and executioner."

Monty threw the gravity well at Nick, who disappeared, but not before releasing his orb. The mages behind him blasted their orbs at us, and the station exploded into flame.

TWELVE

BEING IMMORTAL MEANS I don't die. There's no coverage in that condition for pain, though. I felt pain just like anyone else. I don't enjoy it. Most of the time I tried to actively avoid situations with high pain potential.

Working with an angry mage had a way of increasing the rate of those situations. The fact that Monty went around pissing off other magic-users wasn't my fault. I grabbed Peaches and pressed the main bead on the mala as the group lifted their rifles and fired. Their bullets never reached us. I peeked around the shield and saw the group of tunnel dwellers unconscious and sprawled out on the platform.

"That was clever," Nick said from behind me. I turned half a second too late, as an orb of air slammed into my side, launching me across the station. Peaches leaped and landed on nothing as Nick disappeared again.

"Monty, he's plane-weaving," I grunted from my side

of the station. I winced in pain as I stood slowly. My body flushed hot as it began to repair the damage. "That pendant he's wearing must be an amplifier of some kind."

Monty made his way over to the mages lying on the floor, and pulled off each of the pendants they wore. After a few seconds, he put them in his pocket and traced a rune in the air. Peaches disappeared a second later.

"What happened? Where did Peaches go? Did your spell disintegrate him?"

Monty held up a finger. "One second," he said, removing the second pendant from the other mage. "He will be back momentarily."

Nick appeared in the station a few seconds later, and rolled on the ground with a very large, angry hellhound clamped onto his leg.

"Let go of him, boy," I said, and Peaches released Nick. I fired Grim Whisper several times. The reaction to the persuaders was immediate, and Nick started convulsing. After about a minute, his body calmed down. "I think Nick is going to stay with us for a moment, Monty. We can have that conversation now."

Peaches snuffled and padded away from the prone and pungent Nick.

"I really hate you right now, Simon," Nick slurred as he shifted into a seated position. "My clothes are ruined."

"Nick, don't take it personally, it's just business." I holstered Grim Whisper. "It's not like you tried to have us shredded or anything. Be thankful those weren't entropy rounds."

"Entropy rounds? You wouldn't *dare*—those are banned," Nick answered indignantly.

"Are you kidding me?" I said, reaching for my gun again. Monty stepped in front of me and crouched down to look at Nick. "Just let me shoot him—a little."

"Where did you get these runed rounds, Nicholas?" Monty said, ignoring me, and pulled out the LIT round to once again show it to Nick. "Allow me to present you with your options: You can answer me, I can let my partner shoot you again, or his pet can have you for a snack—your choice."

Monty reached down, removed the pendant from Nick's neck and placed it in his pocket with the others.

"I'm just a middleman." Nick held up his hands. "Like you said, I don't deal in contraband ammunition. It's too much of a headache. Especially LIT rounds. Too much heat with those."

"Bullshit," I said, drawing Grim Whisper, which caused him to scurry back away from me. "Let me shoot him again a few times."

"Nicholas," Monty said, calmly holding up three fingers, "I only need three pieces of information from you. Who runed them? Who procured them? And how much were you paid?"

"I'm telling you I don't know who made them," Nick said. Monty frowned, shook his head, and turned to me.

"Simon, what do you think your creature will remove first…arms or legs?" Monty asked. "He'll have to be treated for consumption of a toxic substance, but maybe if he takes small bites?"

"Wait! Wait," Nick pleaded. "You said three things. I

can tell you the other two."

"The rounds were picked up by a group of Blood Hunters," Nick said, the words tumbling out fast. His eyes never left Peaches, who rumbled at him. "I only spoke with one of them, but she was dangerous. They called her Stasi."

"How much did this Stasi pay for the rounds?" Monty said as he clenched his jaw. "It had to be enough for you to deal with the 'heat' of the Dark Council."

"It was." Nick smiled. It was a greasy, slimy thing that made me want to shoot him again. "Oh, it was."

"How much?" I said, angry. "How much money did she give you?"

"It wasn't money," Nick whispered, and looked away. "She paid in blood—vamp blood. Ten vials of it."

THIRTEEN

"YOU'RE TRAFFICKING REDRUM? You filthy piece of—" I started, but Monty reacted faster than I did. Nick flew across the station, slamming into the far wall, cratering it.

Nick slid down the wall in a crumpled heap. "What are you, a vamp-lover?" he groaned, spitting blood as he spoke. "They're just vampires. They deserve to die."

I holstered Grim Whisper. Every part of me wanted to put an entropy round in his chest and call it a day. Monty must have sensed it because he stepped close to me. I stepped around him and approached Nick.

"It was above board," Nick said quickly, and wobbled to his feet. "I didn't ask for it, but that's what she gave me. It's worth ten grand a vial on the street. She gave me ten vials just to hand over some rounds—so you do the math."

"Do you know how many people that poison has killed?" I said, trying to keep my rage in check. "I'm not going to waste a round on you, Nick. No, I'm going to make a call, and let the vampires know you're carrying ten vials of Redrum. That should make them eager to pay you a visit. What do you think?"

He visibly paled at my words. "Simon, c'mon, it's just business," he said, holding up his hands in surrender. "Don't do this. They'll kill me."

"How do you think they got the ten vials, Nick?" I snapped back. "You think some vampire donated the blood?"

"Do you know where the Blood Hunters are currently?" Monty asked as he placed a hand on my shoulder.

Nick shook his head. "I can make this right. This is more trouble than its worth," he said while he gestured. I drew Grim Whisper, and Monty moved faster than I could track. A lattice of golden energy fell over Nick and pinned him to the ground. "Here, take them. This is too much heat. There was no way I was going to be able to move them."

Nick held a small, ornate box in his outstretched hand. Monty removed it slowly. It was made of lapis lazuli and was elegantly designed with gold filigree on each of the corners. I could see the runes inscribed on its surface glowing softly.

"This is a keepsaker box." Monty examined the box for a few seconds before opening the lid. Inside, I could see the vials filled with a dark red, almost black liquid.

Nick shrugged and slowly got to his feet as the lattice vanished. "That's what she gave me, and I'm giving it to you."

"Nicholas," Monty said, peering up to look at Nick,

"the Council and the sects turn a blind eye because of the services you provide to the magic community. They consider you a necessary evil."

Nick nodded and bowed. "I try to be of service."

"If I find that you are dealing in this filth again—I won't turn a blind eye," Monty said, his voice steel. "I will come here and erase your little world, before handing you over to the Tribunal."

"No. No need," Nick said hurriedly. "From now on I'll stay away from that vile liquid—you have my word. I'll only deal in the good illegal items, not the ones that can get me killed."

He stepped back, gestured, and disappeared along with the homeless dwellers. We stood alone on the station platform.

"We're back to square one," I said with a sigh. "The Tribunal you threatened him with—isn't that the same Tribunal after you for the void vortex?"

"Your point?" he said, holding up the box. "We are going to have to use a circle to exit the Market."

I groaned. "I don't think my body can take that trip. How about just leaving the way we came?"

Monty glanced at me. "Do you trust Nicholas?" he asked, still examining the surface of the box. "Do you think he's just going to let us leave without trying to get this back? We need to get this blood to Haven."

I nodded. "Good point. Fine, let's do the timewarp again," I said and gestured that he should make the circle. "Create it."

Monty looked at me, confused. "Timewarp? It's a simple spatial displacement spell—like taking a jump to the left or a step to the right. There's no temporal component required for it to function."

I just stared at him. Peaches bounded up next to me, while Monty shook his head and created a teleportation circle around us. I took a deep breath as the runes flared and the world slid sideways.

FOURTEEN

WE REAPPEARED OUTSIDE of the Hudson Yards Station. I managed to take a step toward the Goat before my intestines knotted up and doubled me over. Whatever food I still had in my body found itself on the sidewalk.

I dry-heaved and caught my breath. "Teleportation sucks," I said between gasps. Monty handed me a napkin. "Why aren't *you* vomiting up everything?"

He stepped back and looked at me. "I've acclimated. It takes a few years of traveling this way to develop a tolerance to the nausea."

I dry heaved, and got myself under control. "I don't see Peaches suffering, and he hasn't had years to *acclimate*," I said, staring at my dog.

<*Why are you wasting food?*>

"Your *creature*," Monty said, looking down at Peaches, "is not from this world. Besides, the way he eats, I don't think anything *can* give him an upset stomach. If it even possesses one. I'm inclined to think he's bottomless."

I felt better and managed to stand up with the assistance of the wall. After a few uneasy steps, I wobbled over to the car and grabbed the door handle. It unlocked with a clang. I opened the door for Peaches, who bounded in. I eased into the driver's seat, closed my eyes, and rested my head back for a few seconds.

I started the engine and let the deep purr wash over me. I cracked open an eye, glancing in the rear-view mirror at my sprawled-out monster hound. "I wasn't wasting it. The circle made me throw up."

Monty stepped in and strapped on his seatbelt as I finished answering Peaches. He gave me a look and grabbed one of his mage powerbars. "You're explaining your nausea to your dog?"

I nodded, threw the car in gear, and got on 34th Street. I was almost back to normal, except for the bitter aftertaste of bile lingering in my mouth and coating my tongue. "He asked."

"Of course he did," Monty said, giving me another look and sitting back. "Something was off at the Market. Nicholas wasn't as cagey as usual."

"He did try and kill us," I said. "He did seem a little *too* cooperative though."

"We didn't learn much, but we may have learned enough." Monty pulled out the keepsaker, examining it.

"The Market was a waste of time. You should've let me just shoot Nick," I said, frustrated, as we drove across the city to Haven. "We're no closer to who created the LIT rounds, and these Blood Hunters are out there targeting Chi. Who the hell are they? And why attack now?"

Monty tapped his chin in thought. "He gave up the vials too easily. Nicholas wouldn't part with a street value of one-hundred thousand that easily—unless…"

"Unless that slimy piece of scum has more," I added. "We need to close the Market down. Let me call the Council."

Monty held up a hand. "Not yet," he replied while looking out the window. "We still have a use for Nicholas and his Market."

"What about the vials we have?"

"Roxanne should be able to determine where this blood came from." Monty turned the keepsaker in his hands. "It wasn't a total waste of time. Very few people can make a box like this. It's a lost craft."

I glanced at him. "Can you track down who made it?"

He rubbed his chin and nodded. "I will need to make some calls, but I think I can narrow it down."

"Now you're talking," I said. "You remind me of that awesome literary detective when you get all pensive like that."

He put the box down and adjusted his seatbelt. "I'm certain you are referring to Holmes or Poirot, yes? I'll even take Miss Marple."

"I said the *awesome* literary detective." I heard a rumble, and glanced into the back seat where Peaches stood with his head out the window. "There's only one Dark Knight."

"Is this the same Dark Knight who runs around in his underwear, with unresolved psychological issues about his parents and only comes out at night?" Monty gave me an eye-roll with a sigh. "One of his missions should be to see a therapist. How you manage to compare Holmes to a cross between Zorro and the Scarlet Pimpernel is beyond me."

"Scarlet Pimple sounds like a bad skin condition," I answered as we pulled up in front of Haven. "But I don't think your violin playing, cocaine addicted, antisocial psychopath is a healthy role model."

"Touché." The hint of a smile crossed his lips. "Let's go see your vampire."

<*I smell bad people.*>

I glanced in the rear-view mirror again. "That's probably just me, boy. My stomach just did the teleportation tango."

"What is it?" Monty asked, alert. "What did he say?"

"Says he smells bad people."

"You certainly have a unique pungency about you," Monty said, looking at Peaches. "And we are close to Haven. Can you ask him what kind of bad people?"

I just stared at him.

"What? That is a perfectly legitimate question," Monty replied to my look. "It would help to know what kind of smell he associates with bad people."

"You want me to ask him what kind of bad people he smells? Really?" We both stepped out of the car. "What is he supposed to answer to that? Maybe I should ask him how every bad thing smells. Would be great to know what a dragon about to roast you smells like."

I stepped over to open the door for Peaches, when a white-hot burst of searing pain shot up my leg. I took half a second to admire the arrow buried in my leg, when a gust of air punched me in the back, stealing my breath. The momentary lack of oxygen was the only thing that prevented me from screaming in agony.

I shot forward, landing unceremoniously near the rear of the car. Two more arrows buried themselves in the asphalt where I'd stood moments earlier. I reached out and slammed the door closed, keeping Peaches inside. I scrambled back and dived to the other side of the Goat as two more arrows bounced off the car.

I sat on the ground with a grunt and tried not to move my throbbing, shish-kebabed leg.

I clenched my jaw against the wave of pain, and banged my head against the car. "Shit! Who the hell uses arrows?" I grabbed my thigh when another tsunami of pain slammed into me.

Monty narrowed his eyes and peeked over the top of the Goat. He ducked back down quickly as an arrow bounced off the top of the car. "Blood Hunters. They must have tracked us from the apartment and the Market. Why didn't they shoot you with a LIT round?"

"Your compassion is breathtaking," I said, trying not to move my skewered leg. "Why did they shoot me at all?"

"They must have followed your vampire to the Moscow. It doesn't make sense, though. If they thought you were a vampire—"

"Why not put me down with a LIT?" I finished. "Can't you put up a shield or something? They're just arrows."

Monty looked at the arrow and shook his head. "A shield would only activate them. These aren't ordinary arrows."

Peaches gently nudged the door behind me and rocked the car from side to side. Monty reached over, opening the door for Peaches. He bounded out, entering 'attack and shred' mode, and stood next to me with a low growl. He looked up and across the street. The growl intensified.

<I can smell them. They hurt you. Can I hurt them back?>

I grabbed Peaches by the scruff of the neck. "Stay here, boy. We don't know who they are."

The arrow in my leg was a nasty piece of work. The fletching was made of red feathers. Along the metal shaft, I could faintly see glowing runes. The head seemed to be some kind of black crystal.

I let out a long breath and shook my head. "This thing is runed. I take back what I said about ordinary arrows."

I grabbed the shaft to pull the arrow out. Monty held my hand, stopping me. "I would advise against that if you want to keep your leg attached to your body. I don't know if your curse involves restoring missing body parts—would you like to find out?"

"What?" I let go of the arrow. "These things explode?"

Monty nodded grimly. "It's a blood arrow. The runes mix with the blood of the victim," he said, pointing at the shaft. "Once exposed to the air, it catalyzes a sudden explosive reaction. You go boom along with the arrow."

"Fuck," I whispered. "Can you disable the runes?"

"I can try," he said after a pause. He rubbed his chin, and examined the arrow closely. "I've never had to remove one of these before. I still don't understand why they didn't just shoot you with a LIT round."

"Stop trying to cheer me up and get this thing out of my thigh," I said and slid over to prop my leg up. "Do I have to say I'd rather keep my leg *attached* to my body?"

"Duly noted." Monty narrowed his eyes. He started tracing runes in the air. I felt the shift in air pressure and looked up.

"Monty, that feels like a—"

An explosion rocked the top two floors of the medical wing.

"Chi," I whispered as my chest became tight.

"I'm sure Roxanne has things under control." Monty pulled me to my feet as he cast a shield. No arrows came at us as we headed for the entrance to Haven. "That arrow makes sense now."

I shuffled to the front entrance of the medical building. I grunted in pain with each step. "They weren't trying to stop us, just slow us down," I said through clenched teeth.

He nodded as he propped me up. "They must know about your healing ability," he said, shoving open the door. "A LIT round wouldn't delay you like this blood arrow."

"Which means someone fed them information," I said, wiping the sweat from my eyes. "Information that's supposed to be classified."

"I'm certain the Dark Council has access to that information," Monty said, making sure Peaches came in behind us before dropping the shield. "They aren't fond of you."

"Us," I countered. "They aren't fond of *us*. Especially after what you did to Beck. I'm positive you're on their shitlist."

The lobby was a hive of activity as we headed to the elevators. Monty had to show credentials several times before they let us head upstairs. We caught the next elevator up. I closed my eyes, leaning my head against the cool metal, as the soft chime indicated each floor we ascended. The pain in my leg had gone down from 'deafening roar' to 'angry hiss' but it wasn't gone completely. I thought about Master Yat.

"Pain is not weakness leaving the body, Simon," he said.

"Especially when you are the one giving the pain…it tends to stay and set up camp," I answered, rubbing the bruises forming on my legs.

A few more thwacks made my point.

"Stop being a smart-ass and listen. You will feel pain. You need to accept this truth."

"I work with an angry mage, and train with Torquemada. Pain is kind of part of the package."

He nodded. "When it comes, accept it. Embrace it. Realize it's a sensation like any other. The same as being hot or cold. Put it to one side and do what must be done. Don't let it overwhelm or control you…ever."

The throbbing in my leg reminded me the blood arrow had skewered my thigh. After a few more concentrated breaths, the pain was gone. The elevator came to a stop several levels below the affected floors. When the doors opened, armed personnel approached and asked us for ID a few more times, until Peaches' growl began to convince them it was a bad idea to get close to us.

"He hasn't had his afternoon nap, so he gets cranky," I said apologetically. "We need to get upstairs."

Several of the guards pointed to the stairwell, while staring at the large hellhound taking up most of the hallway. I swear he made himself appear larger.

<*I'm not cranky. I'm hungry. Did you bring snacks?*>

"Snacks? Do you see the arrow in my leg? No. I don't have snacks for you."

<*I see it. That isn't a snack. At least not a good one. Do you want me to take it out of your leg?*>

"No, thanks," I said, pushing open the stairwell door. "Monty has to disable it first."

Monty shook his head. "You need to either stop talking to your creature in public, or learn to speak to him silently."

"He didn't come with an instruction manual," I shot back. "So unless you know how to speak mental hellhound, I'm open to suggestions."

Monty narrowed his eyes at me. "I've noticed *you* get to call him a *hellhound*, but you make it a point to stress his name if anyone else calls him that."

I waved his words away. "Good to see they've increased the security," I said, looking behind us at the guards. "Makes me wonder how the explosion happened in the first place?"

"We need to get upstairs," Monty said, giving me a concerned look. We entered the stairwell, and Peaches gave me a nudge. "Will you be able to take the stairs?"

"No choice, let's go."

FIFTEEN

I TOOK THE stairs one at a time, with Peaches bringing up the rear—literally.

"You don't need to shove me, dog," I said after a particularly gentle push that nearly smashed me against a wall. I caught Monty smiling. "Glad this is entertaining you."

"Your condition fills me with the utmost concern," Monty answered but wouldn't look me in the face. "I have a theory about the explosion, but I don't think you're going to like it."

"Please expound, oh wise and knowledgeable mage," I said with a flourish and then wished I hadn't. I grimaced in pain. A white-hot jolt of agony shot through my leg as Peaches gave me another nudge.

"Serves you right, you bloody arse," Monty said. "Do you want to hear the theory or not?"

The pain had rendered me speechless. I motioned for him to continue as I caught my breath.

"How do you capture the head of the Dark Council

without starting an all-out war?" he asked as we climbed another flight of stairs.

"You don't. It's too risky," I answered between gasps. Trying to keep the pain at bay was taking most of my concentration. "Trying to kidnap her would be an act of war no matter who did it. Plus, then you have a pissed-off Chi. I wouldn't wish *that* on anyone. Besides, there's no easy way to get to her."

He nodded. "True, but if she becomes critically injured she would be moved to a supernatural medical facility."

"Which still has top-level security," I said, shaking my head. "I don't see where you're going with this. Why would they want Chi?"

"I don't know the answer to that—yet," he said as he pulled open the door. "What if other vampires were attacked by Blood Hunters tonight? Not with LIT rounds but with blood arrows?"

I followed his train of thought after a pause. "If we have a bunch of vampire-kebabs in Haven, all it takes is one person to pull out a blood arrow—"

He nodded as we stepped into the narrow hallway. "Instant distraction," he said as Roxanne approached us with a black envelope in her hand. "Try not to overreact, Simon."

"Why would I overreact—?"

Roxanne DeMarco, the director of the facility—and a sorceress—was a tall, slim brunette with deep green eyes that you could get lost in if you stared too long. There was a small scar across her forehead and plenty of new scratches and cuts courtesy of the recent explosions.

"I'm so sorry, Simon," Roxanne said, her voice tight with emotion. "The explosion was a diversion. Someone pulled a blood arrow without de-activating it first. Whoever did it detonated part of the infirmary, the other vampires, and themselves. By the time we realized what had happened—she was gone. We found this."

She handed me the envelope. My vision tunneled in as I realized they had taken Chi. I clutched the arrow in my leg, but Monty reacted faster than I could, stopping me.

"Monty, get this arrow out of my leg or I'll take my chances and pull it out myself," I said through clenched teeth, trying to keep the rage in check. I opened the envelope. The small card inside was covered with red runes. I handed it to Monty. "What does it say?"

Monty looked up at me and then at Roxanne. She nodded.

He cleared his throat. "'Return the dark blades or we will release the vampire to the sun,'" he said, turning the card over. "These numbers look like coordinates."

"What dark blades?" I asked, confused. "Release to the sun—they're going to kill Chi if we don't give them these blades?"

Monty shook his head. "We need to get that arrow out of you—now," he said as he flexed the muscles of his jaw.

"Take him to the MRI department. Morphology is the most shielded room on this level," Roxanne said, placing a hand on my shoulder. "We'll get her back, Simon. I give you my word."

"Thank you," I said, not trusting my voice to say

more. "You may want to clear this floor in case Monty gets this disabling thing wrong."

"Isn't that room locked?" Monty asked, propping me up and heading down the hallway. "What's the combination?"

"We had to redo the runic shields after your powershift," Roxanne replied while keeping pace with us. She touched his arm and we stopped. "The new combination is 692017153, along with your palm print. You only have one try. Make sure it's correct."

"What happens if he messes it up?" Monty shot me a look. "Hypothetically speaking, of course."

"The lockdown failsafe is designed to keep high-level entities secure in the room." Roxanne looked at Monty. "If you input the wrong code, the entire morphology wing is quarantined. You'll be trapped in the MRI room on a timed-release protocol."

"How long?" I asked, patting my pockets for a pen and trying to remember the nine digits. "How long does it last?"

"Forty-eight hours," she answered grimly and removed a pen from her lab coat. "In addition—"

"In *addition*?" I said, taking the outstretched pen from her and writing down the code on my palm. "There's more?"

She nodded, ignoring my interruption. "The ventilation system will cycle through several neuroinhibitors—some of which are toxic to humans," she said, stepping back. "Don't input the wrong code. Do you remember the combination?"

Monty nodded as he propped me up. "Palm print and the nine digits you gave us," he said. "Simon was right. I've never dealt with a blood arrow in this manner. It may be best to clear the wing."

Roxanne hesitated a moment. "Do you need me to go with you?" she offered. "I could get you into the room."

"No," Monty said quickly. "No, I need you to look into something else." He searched his jacket pocket and pulled out the keepsaker. The runes covering the blue box gave off a faint glow.

"A keepsaker?" Roxanne said, the surprise evident in her voice. She took the ornate box from Monty and examined it. "This one is exquisite. What is it holding? Can it be opened?"

Monty nodded. "Vampire blood. I disabled the protective runes," Monty said, pointing to the surface. "Ten vials used as payment for LIT rounds, or at least their exchange. I need to know if they all belong to the same vampire. Check with the Smiths."

"LIT Rounds, vampire blood and these bloody arrows," Roxanne said, gesturing at my leg. "What are you two mixed up in? I'm sorry. That was uncalled for and none of my business."

Monty looked at her, narrowed his eyes, and turned away. He always had trouble explaining why he did the things he did. He risked his life when it would have been easier to walk away.

The one time I'd asked him, he'd given me a typical Montyesque answer: "Power must be used to benefit others. Not kept hidden away on some mountaintop." I never felt the need to ask him again.

"Oh, the usual," I cut in with a smile. "I'm sure Monty has pissed off someone or something and now they're coming to erase us."

"That's not funny, Simon," she whispered. "Promise me you'll be safe, Tristan."

Monty looked at her and shook his head. "No, I can't promise we'll be safe. I promise we'll be careful."

Roxanne crossed her arms. "I suppose that'll have to do." She pulled out her phone. "I'll get the wing cleared out. Go take care of that arrow without blowing yourselves to bits—please."

Monty nodded as we headed to the door separating the wings. Peaches rumbled next to me and I motioned for Monty to stop a second.

"Can you keep Peaches with you?" I said, looking back at Roxanne. Peaches sat on his haunches behind me. "If this goes south I don't want him in there with me."

Roxanne gave me a look. "How exactly would you like me to achieve that? Do you carry lengths of chain with you?"

"Give me a second." I held up a hand to her as Peaches nudged into me, nearly knocking me down. "Hey, boy, I need you to stay with Roxanne. We'll be right back."

<*No. You're hurt. I will stay with you until you are better.*>

"We're going to do something pretty dangerous and I don't want you to get hurt," I said, rubbing his head. "You'll be safer here with her."

"Is he talking to the beast?" Roxanne asked Monty as she stepped closer. "Does it speak back?"

Monty nodded. "Apparently it sounds like Vinnie Jones, but only Simon can hear the voice"—he made a circular gesture with his finger near his temple— "in his head."

"Not helping," I muttered under my breath.

"Well, it's true, you're the only one who can hear it," Monty answered. "I almost feel sorry for the creature, only being able to communicate with you."

"Peaches, stay here, with Roxanne." I tried using my best Darth Eastwood voice. In my head, it was a gravelly cross of menace and sternness. He must have heard it differently though, because he snuffled and I could swear it was a laugh. He shook his head.

<*Where you go, I go. And I'm hungry.*>

"When aren't you?" I said, looking down at him, exasperated. "Fine, let's go."

"What did he say?" Monty asked, glancing at Peaches. "Wait, let me guess—he's hungry?"

"Hilarious," I snapped as a wave of pain crested in my throbbing leg. "He won't go and we're wasting time. I need this arrow out of my leg…now."

"Probably for the best—I don't have any stray cows lying about to feed it, in any case," Roxanne said as she dialed a number. "I'll get the wing cleared. You make sure you lot come back to me intact."

She went down the corridor and disappeared around a corner. We walked past the doors and headed into the Morphology wing. The hallways were deserted as we approached the main MRI room.

"Do you remember the code?" I asked him as we stood looking at the panel for the palm print. He gave me a withering look and placed a palm on the smooth surface. It scanned his hand and went blank. A second later, a keypad appeared on the screen.

"Of course I remember the code," he said, punching

in the numbers. "It was only nine digits—child's play."

"Who are the Smiths?" I asked as the locks disengaged and the panel flashed a message of runes. Monty pressed a green circle and the panel went dark. A few seconds later the door hissed opened. The immense room was brightly lit, with the MRI scanner dominating the center of the floor.

"Let's get that arrow removed first," Monty said as we stepped inside the room. "Then we can focus on why they want your vampire and these dark blades."

The machine resembled a typical MRI machine except that it was about five times larger and covered in runes. The machine was surrounded on three sides by three-inch Lexan, also inscribed with runes. In this case, MRI stood for morphological runic imagery. There was another pad to the side of the door and Monty repeated the process to lock it from the inside.

"That is one big machine," I said, admiring the sheer size of the scanner. The runes on its surface danced and shifted, changing colors as they moved. "Any reason why they just can't use a normal MRI machine and not this industrial-sized monster?"

"People and beings who wield magic can't be scanned with magnetic resonance," Monty said, pulling out the oversized platform for me to lie down on. "Their bodies give off too much runic 'noise' to be read properly. This machine essentially uses magic to read a magic-user."

"You told Roxanne you had never removed an arrow in this manner," I said as I slid onto the platform gingerly, keeping my leg elevated to avoid hitting the arrow. "How do you usually deal with a blood arrow?"

"During the war, a variation of these arrows was used. We employed a specific strategy called the 'pull and shove' to remove them," Monty said and turned on the MRI scanner. "Pull the arrow out, use a blast of air to shove them back, watch them explode. It was very efficient."

"I thought it was only the arrow that exploded?"

He shook his head slowly. "Once these runes come in contact with blood, they convert the blood around the wound into a liquid explosive similar to nitromethane," he said, tracing runes around the arrow and my leg. "Pulling out the arrow is similar to lighting a fuse."

"Can we not use *that* method? What the hell, Monty?"

"It was war," he whispered as he strapped my leg down. "They were enemy combatants and we didn't have time for niceties. Evils can be created much quicker than they can be cured. Things like this are why I left the Sanctuary."

"Those who could win a war could rarely make a good peace," I said, bracing myself. "I'm glad you're working on the peace part."

"Are you ready?" he asked and gave me a tight smile. "Tell your creat—*Peaches*—to move back, if you can."

Peaches padded back behind one of the large Lexan screens to one side of the MRI scanner.

"Good boy," I said and gritted my teeth against a wave of pain and nausea as Monty grabbed my leg. "Monty, don't blow me up."

SIXTEEN

MONTY NARROWED HIS eyes as he examined the arrow. I was going to ask him if he needed spectacles or whatever mages called glasses. It seemed his vision was going since I was noticing a lot of squinting lately. I figured this wasn't the time to bring up his failing vision or distract him so I made a mental note to bring it up later.

He gestured with his hand and I saw black tendrils encircle the arrow and my leg. The tendrils snaked around the wound and entered my skin. Sweat formed on Monty's brow as he traced more runes.

I let out a long breath against the pain and clenched my fists around the platform. "That looks like Negomancy," I said with a hiss as the pain increased. It felt like Monty had jammed a hot poker into my thigh and decided to wiggle it around. "That—isn't feeling good. In fact it's feeling pretty damn—"

Monty wiped the sweat from his eyes. "It doesn't get better—not yet, at least," he said quickly without taking his eyes off the arrow. "Shut it and let me concentrate. I would rather stop the unstable explosion *before* it obliterates us."

"Before is a good plan. I like before."

He gave me a short nod. "You have to remain still now," he said. "I'm going to remove the arrow and the pain will be magnified."

"Wonderful," I replied, clenching my teeth. "More pain."

"It will feel like your blood is on fire," he added, grabbing the arrow. "Resist the urge to move or squirm or this will get messy."

"Got it," I answered, closing my eyes and taking a deep breath. "Go for it."

He pulled out the arrow and it felt like my body exploded in flame as I screamed. I opened my eyes, expecting to be engulfed in flames, and reflexively reached for my mark—the endless knot inscribed on the back of my left hand that allowed me to stop time for ten seconds. It bound me to Karma and occasionally she made an appearance when I used it. Right now, I just wanted the pain and burning to stop.

Monty grabbed my hand and stopped me, shaking his head.

"We have to let it run its course," he said, strapping my arm down. "Your body's healing should take over now."

The burning sensations radiated outward from my leg and covered my entire body. It felt like being shoved in a sauna with a setting of 'surface of the sun' as the ambient temperature. I looked down at my leg and expected to see the skin melting away from my body.

After what felt like a lifetime, but was closer to thirty seconds, the burning and pain started to subside. "I'm feeling better," I said with a gasp and put my head back against the platform. "The burning is almost gone."

"We may have a problem," Monty whispered, and the platform trembled. "The arrow is still active."

An orange orb of energy floated in front of him. Inside the orb, I could make out the arrow. The runes along the shaft were bright red and pulsing.

I slid off the platform. "What do you mean it's still active?" I moved to the side, giving the orb and Monty a wide berth. "I thought you said it was the blood that exploded?"

"It would seem, in this case, they expected us to attempt a removal and planned for this contingency," Monty said as he backed away with the orb in front of him.

"Can you contain it?"

He shot me a look. "What do you think I'm presently doing?" he said. I could hear the strain in his voice. "If I remove the orb, it explodes."

"How about the MRI machine?" I said, looking at the giant scanner. "Can you put the arrow in there? It looks sturdy enough to take a small explosion."

Monty looked from the machine to me and gave me a slight nod. "Every so often the functioning of your brain surprises even me," he said and shifted the orb to place it in the MRI scanner. The orb floated lazily inside the scanner as we stepped back to the panel next to the door. "We want to be outside of the room. I have a feeling this will cause the scanner some considerable damage."

"You do know Roxanne is going to be pissed you blew up her machine?" I moved next to the door as he placed his hand on the panel. "It's probably expensive too."

"I'll tell her this was your idea," he said, punching the nine-digit code. His hand froze after he punched in the last digit and the screen flashed yellow. A string of runes raced across the top of the screen. I didn't recognize them, but the large flashing skull-and-crossbones in the center of the panel told me something bad just happened. "That's not good."

"Monty, that looks the opposite of good," I said, looking for some place to take cover. "You punched in the wrong code, didn't you?"

"Oh shite," he whispered more to himself. "I must have juxtaposed a digit."

The door behind us flared bright red as runes appeared on its surface. Several bolts slammed into the wall, reinforcing the locking mechanism. Red lights began to strobe above us and I could hear a klaxon going off somewhere. I felt the vibrations of blast doors slamming into place. The entire wing was quarantined.

I turned slowly to face him. "'Oh shite'? 'Juxtaposed,' really?" I asked as he began tracing runes. "How much power will the blood arrow unleash inside of the scanner? What kind of explosion are we looking at?"

He muttered something quickly under his breath, crouched down and began tracing a semi-circle of runes on the floor in front of us. "If my recollection serves me, the explosion of the arrow is equal to about a quarter kilogram of TNT," he said after a few seconds. "The energy output is approximately 1.2 mega joules."

"Your powers of recollection don't inspire much trust at the moment." I stared at him, shaking my head.

"Excuse me for being bloody distracted," he said testily. "I was only removing a volatile arrow from your leg and containing it in an orb designed to prevent it from exploding us into little bits."

I took a deep breath. "I'm sorry and thank you, Monty, really," I said after a moment and then examined the door. It's just that we're in here and Chi is out there—somewhere."

He waved my words away and shook his head. "It's not your fault," he said, reading the runes on the door. "I should've paid attention."

"It's not like I can shoot this door with an entropy round. It looks stronger than the MRI machine," I said, resting a hand on Grim Whisper.

Monty shook his head slowly as he rubbed his chin. "That door could probably stop a gang of ogres without taking a dent."

"What does that mean in terms of us *surviving* the explosion?"

"The outlook is bleak to nil," he said and traced more runes on the floor. "This shield should act as buffer, but I don't like our chances even with your mala assisting the casting."

"Well, I feel much better now, thanks. Guess I'll find out how immortal I am after all," I said and grabbed Peaches, pulling him close. "Exploding to death wasn't on my to-do list today."

"Unfortunately, since the arrow is in the center of the MRI scanner, the explosion will be exponentially greater, closer to five kilograms of TNT," he said, ignoring me. He continued tracing runes and then stood, rubbing his chin again. "Wait…the entropy rounds. Give me one." He stretched out a hand.

I ejected the magazine and removed one of the rounds. Black energy wafted up from it as I placed it in his hand. "I don't see how one round is going to help with an explosion that's going to erase us."

"The round should act as a disruptive force, bifurcating the initial shockwave and allowing us a narrow trench of inverse runic activity," he explained matter-of-factly. "It will require precise manipulation and alignment, but Ziller's theorem of gravitational disruption should apply."

"Is this Ziller person alive?" I asked, thoroughly lost. "Because I would enjoy introducing his head to my fist."

"Professor Ziller resides at the Sanctuary as part of the living library," Monty answered as he completed the semi-circular design on the floor. "If you do meet him, I would strongly advise against any physical violence. He's an accomplished mage in his own right."

"Can you explain what you just said in English I can understand?"

"Stay behind this semi-circle," he said, looking down and gesturing over the round in his hand. Blue runes floated through the air, descending on the entropy round. "The orb will dissolve shortly and the arrow will detonate. Once the orb disappears, you activate your shield."

"Then what?" I pulled on the mala bracelet to have easier access to the main bead. "You just said we had little chance with a regular explosion. How are we going to make it through one ten times worse?"

"One second," he said, holding up his hand. "We're running out of time. Listen."

At first I didn't hear anything over the klaxons, then I caught it. It was a steady hissing.

"Shit," I said, grabbing Peaches and covering his nose with a sleeve. "Neurotoxins. Is that one round going to be enough?"

"If I don't collapse first, we should be fine."

I stared at him. "Oh good, I wouldn't want you overly concerned or nervous," I said, making sure Peaches remained still.

"The entropy round will give us a slight chance to divert the initial crest of the explosion," he said without looking up. The entropy round floated above his hand and rotated slowly until he aligned it to the MRI scanner and the arrow tumbling slowly in its center. "Get ready, the orb is about to fail."

"I'm not even going to pretend to understand what you just tried to explain—again," I answered and grabbed hold of the mala bracelet. The sweat from my hands made the smooth wood feel slick in my fingers. "Ready."

I held my breath as the orb disappeared. Monty muttered something under his breath and the bullet shot off faster than if I had fired it from Grim Whisper. I looked down to make sure I was behind his semi-circle of runes before I pressed the main bead on the mala. The shield shimmered into place as the arrow exploded. There was only one problem. Monty was on the other side of the shield.

SEVENTEEN

I TRIED TO shift to get Monty behind the shield, but my arm was locked in place. The semi-circular design on the floor glowed with a yellow light and exerted pressure on my body, forcing me back. Peaches tried to move but couldn't.

<The wall of light won't let me pass.>

"Me either, boy," I said quickly and tried to push against the shield. Monty stood in front of us and placed his palms together. The shockwave of the explosion was followed by a wall of flame that rushed at us. Monty spread his hands and I seriously had a Charlton Heston flashback as the flames parted and crashed into the wall on either side of us.

Another explosion rocked the MRI machine, reducing it to its component parts. A hole the size of the center of the scanner was blown clean through the Lexan and the wall directly behind it. Monty extended a hand behind him, gestured, and the shield dropped. I felt the tug immediately. We were being pulled into the hole. Walls of flame raged on either side of us as we slid forward. I grabbed Peaches, making sure he didn't slide into the flames. This was worse than being caught in a riptide. At least with a riptide, there was no threat of being charbroiled.

"Stay in the center!" Monty yelled above the roar of the flames around us. "We have a small window. Make sure you ride the runic current or you will end up in the flames. Hurry! That round won't divert the blast forever."

"What? Ride the what?" I yelled back as the pull intensified. We began picking up speed. The blast furnace walls of flame made it impossible to speak. Monty pointed at me with two fingers and then back to his eyes. I nodded.

Monty ran forward and leaped, reaffirming that mages were on the far edge of insane. Whatever current was pulling on us grabbed his body. He floated motionless for a split second before he launched through the hole. I felt a weight against my leg. I looked down to see a frozen Peaches, stiff and unmoving.

<*Can't move. Feel sleepy.*>

I scooped him up with a grunt. "You need to cut the pastrami—for real," I said as I followed Monty. I ran forward, leaped in the air, and twisted my body, making sure my back was to the hole. The current caught me and I stopped moving mid-leap. I barely held on to Peaches as we shot out of the room. We landed in an unceremonious pile and crashed into beds and equipment. When I finally came to a stop, Monty was facing the hole and gesturing.

A large sphere of yellow energy plugged the hole and he motioned for us to move to the far side of the room. He wiped the sweat from his brow and eyes. I could see a trickle of blood from his nose.

"You're bleeding," I said and pointed at his face.

"Move back," he said, pushing me next to some toppled beds. He wiped his nose and used the blood to trace a single rune into the floor in front of the beds.

"What?" I said, breathing hard while moving a few hospital beds into a makeshift cover. "Isn't the explosion done?"

I placed the unmoving Peaches on the floor behind the beds. His eyes were closed and I couldn't tell if he was breathing. I was more concerned about my frozen hellhound than the impending explosion.

"It will be once the entropy round is absorbed," he said and clenched his jaw. "Bollocks, we're too close."

"He's not moving, Monty," I said, quickly placing a hand on his chest. "I can't tell if he's breathing."

"It's the neurotoxins," Monty said, focusing on the yellow sphere. "He should recover now that we're out of there."

The sound of distant thunder filled the room.

"How bad is this going to be?" I asked, moving more debris between us and the hole in the wall.

"I hope this works," he whispered. Monty looked down and placed a hand on the blood rune. I heard him mutter some more words as the sound went from distant thunder to approaching cataclysm.

Movement followed the change in air pressure. We both looked up at the wall with the hole. The sphere plugging the hole began to distort as the wall bulged out toward us. Monty twisted his hand on the symbol he had traced on the floor. The blood rune flared with violet energy as the wall exploded, and Monty screamed.

EIGHTEEN

"MONTY? PEACHES?" I croaked as I opened my eyes and took in the scene. "Where are they?"

I was lying in a hospital bed, which meant I was still in Haven. There was a bustle of EMTe and hospital personnel activity around me, but I didn't see Monty or Peaches. I tried sitting up and a rough hand pushed me back down in the bed. I looked up and saw an EMTe patch.

"EMTe" stood for EMT elite. The NYTF used these paramedics whenever they encountered some kind of supernatural disaster, or when Monty was allowed to run rampant, which was pretty much the same thing. They all wore dark red uniforms and drove around in extra-large blue ambulances.

"Strong, how the hell do you two manage to destroy so much property in such a short time?" said a voice from the head of the bed. "Can you answer that?"

I recognized the rough voice of sandpaper over gravel. He could easily give Sam Elliot a run for his money with that voice.

"Hey, Frank," I said as he came into view. "I don't do the destruction. You need to speak to Monty, the mage of demolition, for an answer."

Frank defined grizzled. Older, in his mid-sixties, built like a wall and probably as tough. He was the oldest EMTe still in the field and was affectionately known as the OG. I thought it meant "old gangsta," but one of the other EMTe told me it meant "original geezer."

"The Morphology wing is gone," Frank answered and pointed at me with his unlit cigar before putting it back in his mouth and chewing. "The *entire* wing."

"What do you mean it's gone?" I asked, propping myself up on my elbows and regretting it immediately as the room tilted. "The explosion wasn't that bad—was it?"

"What used to be the Morphology wing is now a crater, so you tell me if it was bad," he said and did a brief check of my vitals. "You seem to be, as usual, a freak of nature and intact."

"Trust me, Frank, it's a curse not a blessing," I said, taking a chance and swinging my legs over the edge of the bed. "I need to find Monty and Peaches."

"You know what's a curse?" he asked as I grabbed my jacket. The flask with Valhalla Java was still in the inside pocket and I considered taking a sip. I reconsidered when I realized Frank was staring at me.

"What?" I said, snapping back to focus on him. "I really need to go, OG."

"The curse is the amount of paperwork you two create for me and my people," he said as he headed for the door. "Why don't you take a vacation somewhere nice—like Antarctica? Not much to blow up or demolish down there. No collateral damage either."

I put on my jacket and headed to the door. "I'll make sure to schedule it in," I said to his back as he walked away. "Right after we deal with our current situation."

He stopped midstride.

"What current situation?" He turned, chewing on his cigar. "You need to be specific."

I didn't know how much to share with him. The EMTe was an independent group that worked closely with the NYTF and Haven. If I said too much, it could end up putting him in danger.

"I don't know if I should be—" I started.

He held up a hand, interrupting me. "Do you mean the situation where the vampire leader of the Dark Council was taken from this facility?" he said as he pointed at me again with the cigar. "Or the one where we have vampires getting harvested for their blood around the city? Maybe you mean the situation where Redrum is on the streets like never before and racking up a body count faster than we can get to them?"

"Shit," I said, grabbing my phone. "This is getting bad."

"Getting?" Frank replied with a snort. "Getting was days ago, boy. This is officially a shitstorm. You'd best find your partner and go do whatever it is you two do. He's probably in the ICU with that large beast you call a dog."

"ICU?" I pressed the speed dial for Monty as my stomach clenched. "Why would they be in the ICU?" I heard the phone go to voice mail and I hung up.

"You were in a room flooded with neurotoxins," Frank replied, switching the cigar from one side of his mouth to the other. "By all rights you should be a paralyzed basket case right now, not walking around talking to me. Took us hours to vent what was left of Morphology. Knowing you, I'm sure your partner and beast are still around, so go find them."

"I'm on it, Frank," I said, pressing another button on the phone. "Thanks again."

Frank started walking off. "Don't thank me," he said, waving my words away. "Just try not to destroy any more buildings. I'm getting too old for this shit."

I called Ramirez. He picked up on the third ring.

"Strong, where the hell have you been?" he nearly yelled. "I've got the brass, some angry vampire named Ken, and the Dark Council all trying to chew me a new one."

I smiled despite myself. For all his griping, Angel Ramirez was one of the best directors the NYTF had ever had. We recently had a falling out over his last lieutenant, Cassandra, who was killed in the line of duty.

Ramirez did not take losing people well. I didn't blame him. I just gave him the space he needed to process the loss. Eventually we mended our differences, because that's what family does.

"I'm at Haven," I said, trying to get my bearings. I looked around the corridor and realized I didn't know where I was. "Blood Hunters are paying NYC a visit."

A string of Spanish curses followed as he yelled. I held the phone away from my ear until he calmed down. "What the hell are Blood Hunters doing in my city?" Ramirez said, his voice on edge. "Did you bring them here? It's not like I don't have enough to deal with."

"They attacked Chi, but I don't know why," I said, grabbing a wandering nurse. "And no, I didn't bring them here. How would I bring them here?"

"This, coming from the person who tangled with the god of chaos?" Ramirez said with a sigh. "I don't know how you bring them here. I only know you attract disaster like shit and flies."

"Give me a sec, Angel," I said, covering the phone and looking at the nurse. "Where would I find ICU?"

"ICU," the nurse answered and pointed down the corridor. I oriented myself, and headed for intensive care.

"Thank you for that wonderful analogy, Ramirez," I said, returning the phone to my ear. "I feel so much better now."

"I have a flood of Redrum hitting the streets like it's on tap," he answered as I heard his radio squawk in the background. "Do you know how Redrum is produced, Strong?"

"Vampires," I whispered as I walked down the corridor. "They get it from vampire blood."

"Who said you weren't sharp?" he answered. "I have the Dark Council pressuring the brass. They're asking me what I'm going to do about vampires being *harvested*."

"You think the Blood Hunters are behind this?" I asked, checking out another one of the hospital maps —an Escheresque design with the sole purpose of getting people lost to the point of insanity. "It doesn't make sense. Why flood the streets with Redrum?"

"Their entire purpose is to do what?" he snapped back. "They're called Blood Hunters for a reason. We find them, we find the Redrum supplier."

His logic did make sense, but something felt off.

"I think I know where the Blood Hunters are," I said, finding the signs that pointed me to the ICU and picking up the pace. "At least one of them. They want something called the dark blades."

"Grab your mage partner, meet them, and find out where this Redrum is coming from," Ramirez said over the squawking of his radio again. "Where are you meeting them and what the hell are dark blades?"

"Don't know," I said, looking for the card given to me by the Blood Hunters. "Never heard of them before, but I'm going to find out. Can you tell me where this is?"

I gave him the coordinates from the back of the card. I heard the keyboard keys click for a few seconds, followed by a low whistle. "Someone is playing hardball," he said after a pause. "These guys did their homework."

"Where is it?" I said as I approached ICU. "Where do they want to meet?"

"NYTF can't go in with you, officially," he answered, angry. "We even set foot in there, we'll have an *incident*—an ugly one."

"Just tell me where it is," I said, dreading the answer because I knew it could only be one place.

"The Foundry," Ramirez said, his voice tight. "Give me a few days. Let me call in a few favors. Unofficially, I'm sure I can swing a warrant to go in with you."

"Angel," I said, my voice thick, "they took Chi. I don't have a few days. I have to go."

"Strong, I'm sorry they took her," Ramirez said quickly. "Listen to me, don't go in there without backup and I mean without an *army* of backup. Not your mage and that thing you call a dog. I know what she means to you, but you can't—"

"If you know what she means to me then you know I'm not going to wait days," I said, looking into the ICU room and seeing Peaches on a hospital bed. "I have to go."

"Strong, goddammit, Strong—"were the last words I heard before I hung up on him.

Monty and Roxanne were standing next to the bed. Peaches was still and barely breathing. Runes encircled his body, glowing faintly with every shallow breath he took.

"How is he?" I said as the words choked my throat. "Is he—?"

Monty placed a hand on my shoulder. "He's stable, but the neurotoxin hit him hard," he whispered, squeezing my arm. "Roxanne did everything she could. The rest is up to him now."

I stepped close to the hospital bed and placed a hand on Peaches' side. His chest rose and fell slowly with each breath. I looked at Roxanne.

"We'll do our best to keep him stable, but we've never treated this species before," Roxanne said gently. "He is quite unique."

I nodded. "I need you to keep him safe, Roxanne," I said, looking down at Peaches. "I don't care if you need to post someone on him round the clock. Keep him safe."

I stared at her and she stared right back, unwavering. "He will be safe, Simon," she said, her voice firm. "I have information for you both."

"The keepsaker?" Monty said, following Roxanne out of the room. I took one look back at Peaches' sprawled body before one of the nurses blocked my view. "Did you speak to the Smiths?"

Roxanne nodded. "First the blood," she said and produced the ornate lapis lazuli box, handing it to Monty. "It belongs to several ancient vampires and is incredibly potent. Each vial is a mixture of their blood and some chemical agent. This blood can't fall into the wrong hands."

"Do we know who these vampires are?" I looked at the vials filled with the dark liquid. "Can you tell when the blood was taken?"

She shook her head slowly. "That's all we can tell for now," she said and crossed her arms. "I'll have that information for you in a day or so. The blood in those vials is lethal to humans."

"Redrum," I whispered. "Goddamn poison."

Monty took out all of the vials except one and handed them to Roxanne. "We don't need to carry it all with us." He closed the box and gestured. I saw the runes on the surface of the box flare. "The Smiths?"

Roxanne tightened her lips. "Aria agreed to see you, but you have to bring her the keepsaker," she said, clearly bothered. "I don't trust her, Tristan. The Smiths are dangerous."

"We don't have a choice." Monty put the keepsaker in a pocket. "She can tell us who requested the box for the blood."

"I have to coordinate the cleanup here, now that we no longer have an MRI machine or a Morphology department," Roxanne said, looking pointedly at Monty. "I swear your visits here can be taxing and destructive. Perhaps a call next time?"

"I'll make sure the scanner is replaced and I'll cover the cost of the damages, but first things first," Monty said with a nod of his head while looking at me. "We need to locate your vampire. Let's go speak to the Blood Hunters and find out what they want badly enough to risk an all-out war with the Council."

"It's the Foundry," I said with an edge in my voice. "We have no backup."

A sharp intake of breath from Roxanne made us turn. "The Foundry?" she whispered. "You're going alone?"

"No one is insane enough to accompany us," Monty answered, rubbing his chin before the slight hint of a smile crossed his lips. "What else is new?"

NINETEEN

THE FOUNDRY WAS a neutral ground, of sorts, in the sense that most of the people who entered its doors were neutralized and vanished from existence.

Located at 2 E. 91st Street, the Foundry had purchased the property once known as the Cooper Hewitt Museum and created a meeting space and home for the elite criminal magic-user. It boasted state-of-the-art security along with nasty runic defenses designed to erase anyone suicidal enough to attempt an unscheduled visit.

The NYTF never set foot in the Foundry. It had no jurisdiction within its walls. The Dark Council acknowledged its presence but chose not to interfere with its activities. Probably had something to do with the fact that a few members of the Council were also members of the Foundry.

The Foundry, like the Vatican, existed as a de facto sovereign state within the city. Similar to the Vatican, it was controlled by an absolute monarch. In this case an

Arch Mage.

I got on Madison Avenue and headed uptown. The Goat's engine purred and rumbled as we raced to 91st Street. I could see the first rays of light bounce off some of the tallest buildings.

"What are the odds of us getting out of there alive without destroying the building in the process?" I asked as Monty reached for one of his mage powerbars. "I really would like to avoid pissing off Julien."

"We're going there with an invitation," Monty said after a few chews. "I could use a good strong cuppa. These bars taste like the bottom of a hamster cage. See if we can get one over there?"

"The invitation means squat, you know that," I said, pulling off to the side in front of a small restaurant catering to the early morning crowd. "I thought sawdust *was* the main ingredient in those things?"

"If I tried to explain what is in these things, your brain really would melt," Monty said, pointing at me with the half-eaten powerbar as he stepped out of the car. "The usual?"

I nodded as he went to get my coffee and his Earl Grey. I looked in the rear-view mirror, expecting to see Peaches sprawled in the back, before I remembered where he was. My stomach clenched for a second and I promised myself to repay the Blood Hunters in kind for skewering my leg with a blood arrow.

Monty came back a few minutes later, handing me my cup. I pulled out the flask from my jacket, pouring about a spoonful of the Valhalla Java in my coffee. It flared blue as it mixed with the liquid. I took a moment to savor the aroma of the enhanced coffee and then sipped the liquid ambrosia.

"And you talk about *my* fixation with tea?" Monty said, staring at me. "Have you seen yourself drinking coffee? It's practically pornographic."

"This is different. This"—I held up my cup—"*this* is the coffee of the gods—Valhalla Java," I said, taking another sip before pulling the Goat off the curb. "You're just drinking a bunch of boiled leaves. And you didn't answer my question."

Monty's jaw flexed and I could tell the idea of going into the Foundry concerned him. "We need to speak to this Blood Hunter," he said after sipping his tea. "If the Foundry was given as the meeting place, Julien knows. Nothing occurs within the walls of his domain without his approval. Implicit or not."

I glanced sideways quickly. "Are you as strong as he is?" I asked. "I mean, you did level up so maybe you're at his level?"

"It's called a power shift, not leveling up," Monty said, finishing his bar. "This isn't a video game, and the answer is no. Julien is a few centuries older than I am and we are entering his home. A mage is always strongest in his home."

"Can't you just—I don't know—tap into more power or hold some in reserve just in case you need it?"

He gave me the 'are you really that dense?' look and shook his head. "It's a matter of resonance and energy alignment. Plus he probably has power modifiers and dampeners spread throughout the property," Monty answered, pulling out the keepsaker.

I pulled up to the entrance of the Foundry and

turned off the car. "Which means we're screwed if this goes sideways," I said, removing Grim Whisper and Ebonsoul. I placed my hand on the center panel between the seats and it slid back, revealing a large storage space. Monty placed the keepsaker in the space. I placed my weapons next to it.

No one entered the Foundry armed. If I brought both weapons I would have to leave them at the door with Claude. Since I didn't trust Julien, Claude, or the Foundry, this was the best solution. I took a deep breath and stepped out of the car, followed by Monty. He pressed his hand on the Goat and it locked with a clang and orange flare.

"Let's go talk to a Blood Hunter," I said, stepping to the front gate.

TWENTY

CLAUDE STOOD AT the entrance of a large black iron fence.

"*Fils de pute*," Claude spat when he saw us. "What do you want? We *just* finished renovations."

"Look, Monty," I said, pointing at Claude, "he sounds so happy to see us. My French is rusty, but that didn't sound polite. Were you being rude?"

Claude glared at me and crossed his arms. He was a small man with piercing eyes who used his stature to his advantage. An accomplished mage and world-class assassin trained personally by Julien, no one underestimated Claude twice—*if* they survived the first encounter. We didn't like each other much.

"Is Julien in?" Monty quietly asked, and I could feel the power coming off him. Claude must have sensed it too because I saw him stiffen and place his hand on his holster. "We need to have a word."

I raised my hand and slowly pulled the black card from the Blood Hunter from my pocket. Claude was jittery, which made me think the Foundry was on some kind of alert. He looked at the card and his face darkened as he turned it over, reading the coordinates before handing it back to me.

"*Merde*," he muttered under his breath, unlocking the gate. "Come with me."

We stepped through the iron gate and my skin tingled. Behind the gate, a winding path led to the front of the large mansion. I saw the runic defenses inscribed on the ground on either side of the path as we crossed the threshold. I recognized the circles from my last visit to the Hellfire Club.

I nudged Monty. "That looks like an—"

"Oblivion circle, yes," Monty whispered, narrowing his eyes. "These are especially lethal. Avoid them."

"Good idea. I've been meaning to ask you…" I said as we walked along the path around the circles behind Claude, "is your vision getting worse?"

Monty looked at me with an expression of surprise. "My what?" he replied quickly. "What would make you think that?"

I shrugged. "Well, you're pretty old and I'm seeing you squinting a lot lately," I said. "There's nothing wrong with wearing spectacles, or bifocals, or even trifocals, if you need them."

"You do realize that mages can live over three millennia?" Monty said, pinching the bridge of his nose. "My eyes are fine. The 'squinting,' as you call it, allows me to shift visual spectrums and view runic energy clearer."

"I'm just saying, there's no shame in getting old," I reiterated with a squint in his direction. "I'm not an

Blood Is Thicker 123

ageist. Clint has an excellent squint, as does Wolverine."

"Your open-mindedness fills me with comfort, considering you will probably reach an age far surpassing mine," Monty replied with a sigh.

Claude snorted derisively.

"You have something to say, Clyde?" I said, knowing he hated when I called him that. "Please share."

He glared at me and took a deep breath before speaking. I liked to think I helped others work on their patience and tolerance. It's my calling.

"*Oui*," he nodded and glanced at Monty. "You are at most two or three centuries old?"

Monty gave him a brief nod. "Over two, not quite three," Monty answered after a pause.

"*Enfant de bas age*," Claude said with a sneer. "You are still a baby. Julien is four times your age. And dwarfs your power, even with your recent shift."

"Well, this *baby* is still a kick-ass mage," I shot back, angrily. "He's faced serious threats and stopped them."

Claude nodded. "Oh yes, a dragon and a deranged pack of wolves," Claude said with mock seriousness. "Very dangerous to a child. The vortex, however, was quite creative—for an amateur. When will the Circle come for you?"

"Not to mention—" I started as Monty gave me a look, and it became clear. Claude was trying to goad me into giving away information. It almost worked and I shut up before I mentioned Chaos. We reached the main door. It was a huge wooden slab covered in symbols and was glowing faintly with runes.

"What do you wish to mention?" Claude asked suddenly.

"Just that Julien takes his security seriously," I said as Claude stepped to the entrance and placed a hand on a panel. Several bolts could be heard sliding away from the door. "Why does someone so obviously powerful need so much protection? I mean, Julien is close to a thousand years old—what's he scared of?"

The door opened with a slight creak from the weight of the wood. Claude stood to one side, giving me a stink-eye as we entered. He opened a door adjacent to the main entrance.

"Julien fears no one and nothing," Claude said as he led us through the foyer into a large room with walls of dark wood. The partially drawn blinds covered the floor-to-ceiling windows and allowed the morning light to cascade softly into the room, causing the polished wood to glisten.

"Well, that would explain all the security," I said, taking in the runes that covered the floors and ceiling, most of which making no sense to me. Books lined the walls and several desks sat in the center of the spacious library.

"Maybe he should leave the doors open? Turn this place into a museum?"

"Your humor is—how you say—troll?" Claude said, giving me a sharp look.

"The word is *droll*," I said and looked down at him as I spoke. "A troll is a short, stupid, mean creature that guards entrances and bridges, sort of like what you do, Clyde."

He gave me a one-finger salute and proceeded to ignore me. Monty walked over to one of the walls, examining the book spines, and ignored Claude, who sensed the affront and bristled.

Monty wasn't arrogant. It was mostly that he's English and has little tolerance for stupidity and small-mindedness. Claude was both, wrapped in a dangerous package. Many mistook Monty's aloofness as being unaware. They discovered with breath–stealing suddenness how fatal that assessment could be.

"Study is always good for a *debutant*," Claude said with a self-satisfied smile. "I apologize that we do not have a children's section in this library."

"I agree." Monty reached out and pulled one of the books from the shelf. "You have a copy of Ziller's laws of Quantum Entanglement. This is quite rare."

Claude responded with a short laugh. "I doubt a mage at your level can comprehend the complexities of that volume," Claude replied, pulling out another book. "Perhaps this book is more to your understanding."

He tossed the book on the desk near Monty. My hand reflexively moved to my holster before I remembered I'd left Grim Whisper in the car. Monty walked over to the desk and picked up the book.

"Ziller's *Rudiments of Spellcasting*," Monty said, examining the spine. "One should never forget the basics."

"Basic," Claude said, making the word sound like an insult. "That is what you are as a mage, Tristan—basic."

"That will be enough, Claude," a soft voice said from the doorway behind us. "I believe the front gate has been unmanned long enough."

"*Seigneur, pardonne moi*," Claude said quickly. He placed his right fist over his heart and bowed. "I shall return at once." Claude brushed past us and left the library without another word.

Monty slid up to me and put a hand on my arm. "Whatever you do, don't call him—" he whispered as Julien approached the room.

"Jules!" I said with a smile as Julien entered the library. "Good morning. Any chance Clyde can get us some coffee?"

Julien stepped farther into the library. His thin frame wore a black Amosu Vanquish Bespoke over a gray Eton shirt. He was barefoot, as usual. In fact, I had never seen him wear shoes. He reminded me of Gandalf—in a suit. His long white hair, usually loose, was in a braid today.

"You must forgive Claude," Julien said as he motioned to the wait staff behind him with a nod of his head. "He is zealous in his protection of me and this place, but he has lost some of his social graces over the years."

"*Some*?" I snapped back. "He has *no* social grace. Maybe you should change his name to something more fitting, like *Connard*?"

Julien winced as he looked at me with a tight smile. "And to what do I owe the pleasure of your company this morning? Did Claude mention we just finished renovations?"

"Why do you keep bringing up renovations?" I asked, looking around. "We aren't interior decorators."

"I disagree," Julien replied with a nod. "Tales of your destructive redecorations precede you. I believe Haven is undergoing repairs as we speak?"

"That wasn't our fault," I said, looking away. "Well, it

was mostly not our fault."

"Of course it wasn't," Julien answered. "I would prefer if you refrained from your destructive demolitions while you visit—if possible."

I produced the card left by the Blood Hunters. Julien took it, read the front, and turned it over. He handed it back to me, his face expressionless.

"She is not here," he said after a few seconds. "Your vampire is not on the premises."

"I really hope that's true," I said, my voice low and dangerous. "I would hate to find out you had something to do with her kidnapping."

Julien gave me a predatory smile, and my blood froze. "Do not threaten me, Simon," he said, his voice full of quiet menace. "I will erase everything and everyone you hold dear and make you watch while I do it."

"Am I supposed to be scared right now?" Actually, I was close to losing bladder control. If there was a person who could make that threat and keep it, it was Julien.

"Your recklessness along with your poor self-control will get you killed one day, Simon," Julien whispered, staring at me.

"Where is the Blood Hunter?" I said when I found my voice again. I really had to stop pissing off people who could squash me with a thought. "And why is she here?"

"I am a facilitator," he answered and removed a cup from the tray on the desk. He gestured for us to do the same. I grabbed a cup of coffee while Monty picked up the tea. I noticed he didn't drink any. "They wanted somewhere to meet where they could feel safe. The Dark Council neutral zones made them uncomfortable."

"Especially when you attack the leader of the Dark Council and then kidnap her," I said after sipping my coffee. "I would be uncomfortable too."

"Please, follow me." Julien led us out of the library and up a grand staircase to the second floor. "It is my understanding that this is to be an even exchange," Julien said as he headed down the central hallway. A set of double doors waited for us at the far end.

"They want something called the dark blades," I said once we reached the doors. "Do you know what they are?"

"You don't?" Julien answered, giving me a curious look. "This isn't recognized neutral ground. That being said, as sovereign of the Foundry it is my responsibility to inform you that an attack on the premises constitutes an act of aggression and will be dealt with harshly. You are here to have a conversation—not a battle."

"What if they attack first?" I said, knowing that this *conversation* could go either way. "What is the protocol? Just in case."

Julien stared at me for a good ten seconds. "All parties involved in the aggression will be terminated, *just in case*," Julien said, nodding at the doors. They slid open silently as he disappeared.

TWENTY-ONE

MONTY AND I entered what appeared to be a sitting room except in extra-large. The same wood from the library adorned the interior of this room. Large chaise lounge chairs sat on either end of the room next to the walls. In the center of the room, several smaller lounge chairs were positioned around a table. An immense fireplace dominated one wall with a loose semi-circle of smaller chairs facing it.

Runes covered the four walls, ceiling, and floor. They flowed and slid over the surfaces, a moving mosaic of energy and power. Julien really was serious about his security.

Near the fireplace stood a woman dressed in what appeared to be a black bodysuit. It was overlaid with sections of ballistic armor that covered parts of her body. Her face, neck, and arms were covered with some kind of camouflage paint. It gave the impression of being dipped in black ink. Her black hair was cut short on the sides and spiky on the top. I did a quick scan and noticed the absence of weapons. She gazed at us, doing her own threat assessment, and approached the center of the room. The way she moved told me that she was lethal—armed or not.

I tossed the card on the table. "Where is Michiko?"

"I see you managed to keep your leg," she answered, picking up the card. "Where are the blades?"

I reached reflexively for Grim Whisper again before I remembered it was in the car. "That was you," I said, flexing my jaw and wishing I had my weapons.

She nodded with a small bow. "We needed to keep you occupied while we extracted the head of the Dark Council," she answered and threw the card back on the table. "I looked forward to your explosion. Defeating a blood arrow means you have some skill."

"Sorry to disappoint," I answered as the anger unspooled inside of me. "You should've aimed higher."

"Next time, I will," she said, crossing her arms. "Did you bring the blades?"

"I need to see Michiko first." I stepped to the right of the table and kept the fireplace on my left. "How do I know she's still alive?"

She sniffed the air. "You smell like her," she said, looking me over and narrowing her eyes. Her voice had a slight accent I couldn't place. "You are not dead or alive. You are her thrall?"

"Her what?" I asked, taking a step forward. "Where is she?" I felt Monty step close to me as the anger rose.

"Who are you?" Monty asked, placing a hand on my arm. "Name and rank."

"I am Estilete. You may call me Esti," she said, still looking at me. "Second to Anastasia Anyxia Santiago,

Blood Is Thicker

leader of the *Cazadoras Sangrientas*. And you are?"

"Tristan Montague of the Golden Circle," Monty answered with a nod. "Why are the Blood Hunters in this city, Esti?"

"The dark blades, *Mago*." She stepped to the side and held up two fingers. "Stolen by the *Karitori-fu*—the reaping wind, during the war. We traced them here and demand their return."

"You would risk war with the vampires and the Dark Council over these blades?" Monty stepped to the side and kept himself bladed to her position. I was in the center of an intricate dance of positioning.

Karitori-fu—the reaping wind—was the name given to the terror of night in Medieval Japan. Tales of her exploits became legends. I was sure they still used stories of her in Japan to make children behave. The *Karitori-fu* was a combination of the bogeyman, the monster under your bed, and every creature that inhabited the night rolled into one—except it was real. Michiko used the name during the Supernatural War.

"We are Blood Hunters," Esti replied, the hint of a smile crossing her face. "Vampires are of no consequence to us." She continued stepping to her right and, frankly, it was making me nervous.

"Why did you attack her?" I asked, shifting to the side and stepping closer to the immense fireplace.

"You care about her?" Esti sniffed the air again. "Do you—*love* her?" she asked derisively.

"We have an—understanding," I said, suddenly uncomfortable discussing my feelings. I could feel Monty gathering power, which made no sense. Julien would blast us to unrecognizable little bits if we disregarded his warning.

"An understanding?" Esti scoffed with a short laugh. "You understand nothing. She is a vampire. You are a meal to her, nothing more."

"You're wrong," I whispered. "Michiko would never feed off me."

"Am I?" Esti flicked her wrists and two long runed blades materialized in her hands. I recognized the runes as the same ones on the blood arrows. Getting stabbed by one of those would end badly. "Do you think your *understanding* will prevent her instincts from taking you? Where are the blades?"

"This is why I hate these *conversations*, Monty," I said, reaching slowly for the flask of Valhalla Java. "No one wants to just converse anymore." I took a long pull from the flask. The skulls on the surface coruscated with blue energy as I felt the liquid burn on the way down. My heart raced and my vision tunneled as a roar filled my ears. This may have been a bad idea.

"Conversation is a lost art," Monty said and formed an orb of air in his hand.

"And this one is over," Esti said as she flicked her wrists and sent her blades at me.

The Valhalla Java, aside from being the best coffee I've ever tasted on this planet, enhanced my reflexes, strength, and vitality for a short time. I hadn't had a chance to test all of its properties. Since it was a gift from Hel, the Norse goddess of the underworld, I was certain there were some nasty side effects to drinking too much of it—like spontaneous explosion or rapid disintegration.

I dived over the table, causing her to miss, and slid in

front of the fireplace. The blades sailed across the room right at Monty. He deflected them with a blast of air, burying them in the far wall. Esti extended her arms and two more blades materialized in her hands. I stood and noticed that the wall above the fireplace began bulging; never a good sign.

I took a few steps back from the expanding fireplace. I shook my head, trying to clear the image of the ballooning wall. Maybe the Valhalla Java had destroyed some brain cells and this was the result. I stood there, transfixed, as the wall got closer. I felt the pressure on my arm and looked down as Monty yanked me to the side. The wall, fireplace, and half the floor exploded into the sitting room.

TWENTY-TWO

"OH SHIT, JULIEN is going to be so pissed," I muttered as I brushed off the debris from the destruction. I looked out of the gaping hole and onto Fifth Avenue. The fireplace was gone. I turned to see Monty tracing runes in the air. I pointed at the wall. "Did you do that?"

His face was tight with concentration. "We need to vacate the premises," Monty said, his voice grim. "This should buy us some time."

Orange energy blossomed, covering the doors and windows. I searched the room for the Blood Hunter, but she was gone. The door to the sitting room vanished, revealing a scowling Julien with a smiling Claude next to him. Julien placed a hand on the orange wall of energy and cursed. If he was angry at his newly ventilated sitting room, the energy wall pushed him into livid territory.

Another explosion outside focused our attention on the hole. "Ordaurum Montague," a voice bellowed from beyond the hole. "By order of the Tribunal of the Golden Circle, you are hereby instructed to surrender yourself to my custody."

"Bollocks," Monty whispered. "They would send *him*."

"That doesn't sound like your pal Gideon," I said, noticing Julien tracing a rune at the doorway. "We can't get out the way we came, and whoever is outside sounds less than friendly. How do you suggest we *vacate* these premises?"

Monty looked in the direction of the large smoldering hole. "That way." He pointed. "Fastest egress."

"You *must* be kidding." I looked out of the hole at the morning traffic racing down Fifth. "We're forty feet off the ground. I'm willing to risk my digestive system for a teleportation circle, because I don't fly."

"No time," Monty said, forming orbs of air. "Julien will disable the barrier at the door at any moment and the Arbiter outside won't remain outside for long. I would prefer to avoid close-quarter runic combat. He's showing Julien a modicum of respect by not attacking us in here, but he's never been known for his patience. Julien, on the other hand, will attempt to erase us once he enters."

"Arbiter?" I groaned and looked at the door. The barrier in front of Julien became fainter by the second. "Couldn't you have just sent the Sanctuary an apology memo promising no more vortex practice in the city?"

"Time to go," Monty said with a quick smile. "Besides, you'll probably only suffer multiple compound fractures—it's not like you're about to plummet to your death."

"Your motivational speeches truly suck, Monty," I said as I ran toward the hole. I leaped out into open space forty feet above the extremely hard New York City sidewalk. An orb of air caught me halfway down and dumped me on the street. I rolled for a few feet before coming to a stop next to the Goat. I scrambled to open the car as a figure landed up the street, cratering the sidewalk.

"You may want to get your weapons now," Monty said from the other side of the Goat as he opened the car door. "This *conversation* is going to be violent."

I jumped into the Goat, grabbing both the Grim Whisper and Ebonsoul. I slid out of the passenger side as the Arbiter walked up the street. I sheathed Ebonsoul and checked Grim Whisper, making sure I had one in the chamber.

"You know him?" I asked as another explosion rocked the top level of the Foundry. "What was that?"

"That was Julien disabling the barriers, and yes, I know him," Monty said, shaking out his hands. "His name is Ian Macintyre and we have—*history*."

The Arbiter casually walked up the street. Where the Envoys looked like renegade wizards escaping a local Ren faire, Arbiters could give Ken a run for his money in the black-on-black wardrobe department. Ian wore a black suit over a black shirt accented by pale gold tie. A small gold circle rested over his left breast. He tapped a walking stick every other step as he approached.

"Gideon is still in intensive care after you shunted him back," Ian said, stopping in the middle of the street. "They say he won't be able to eat solid food for months."

"I did warn him," Monty said, stepping into the street. "You should go back, Ian."

"Warning me now, are you?" Ian replied as he rested both hands on top of his walking stick. He stood with his legs slightly apart and narrowed his eyes at me. "Tell your friend that if he interferes, I'll kill him—repeatedly."

"Stay back, Simon," Monty said as he flexed his fingers. "He's dangerous."

Across from Monty on the other side of the street slept a homeless man. He was dressed in old rags and what appeared to be a coat of black feathers. He clutched a long thick gnarled branch in his hands. It surprised me that I didn't notice him earlier, but I guess jumping out of a building away from an angry Arch Mage has a way of focusing your attention.

Something about the homeless man set off my radar. I was about to cross the street and tell him to find a safer street to crash in when Ian hit the street with his walking stick. I felt the tremor as it raced toward us. I saw Ian nod and several fireballs blazed down the street at us. Monty threw up a shield and deflected them to either side. One of the fireballs nearly hit the homeless man, who kept on snoring, blissfully ignorant of his impending incineration.

"How did he manage casting without the finger wiggle?" I asked Monty as another wave of fireballs crashed into his shield. "Seems like a useful skill."

"He's powerful, he's old, and he cheats," Monty said, throwing up another shield. "He uses a runed staff to channel additional power as a reserve. It allows him to cast spells without energy manipulation. It makes him fast, unpredictable, and deadly."

"Gideon's mistake was that he wanted to take you back alive," Ian said as he pointed his stick and a chunk the size of the Goat tore free from the sidewalk. It floated lazily just above his head. "He underestimated you—an error I won't repeat."

"You should leave now before I hurt you, Ian," Monty said over the roar of another wave of fireballs. "Tell them you couldn't find me."

"You know I can't do that, Tristan," Ian said and waved the stick forward, hurling the large slab of concrete at us. "In fact, this will be easier if you just let me kill you and bring back your body. We can always train another Ordaurum."

Monty pulled me back and placed a hand on my chest, blasting me with a gust of air and launching me behind the Goat. The concrete slab slammed into and passed his shield. Monty backpedaled and threw up another shield when the slab burst into a dust cloud. I rolled into a ready position with Grim Whisper drawn. I saw the look of surprise on Monty's face, and a matching expression of shock on Ian's.

Julien was walking down the street with a grinning Claude in tow. Black orbs of energy floated in his hands and he looked displeased. I looked across the street but the homeless man was gone. I ran for the Goat.

"I think this is a good time for a strategic retreat," I said as I scrambled into the Goat with Monty pausing to deflect another fireball.

"Agreed," Monty answered as he placed his hands

together. When he pulled them apart, a latticework of orange energy formed between his fingers and expanded as it floated down the street. He jumped in the passenger side. "It would be in our best interests if we were far away when that net reaches them."

I floored the gas pedal and raced the Goat down the street and away from the Foundry as an explosion roared behind us. Flames and runic energy filled the rear-view mirror as I glanced behind us. There was nothing else to see besides devastation.

"Did you kill them?" I asked, keeping my foot glued to the floor. "What did you send at them?"

"Something I'm sure Claude will appreciate," Monty said with a sigh and put his head back in the seat. "I need to go to the Sanctuary."

"What?" I said, nearly losing control of the car. "Aren't they the ones trying to kill you?"

"There is a way we can do it, but we need to go downtown," Monty said, grabbing one of his mage powerbars. "We need to go to the Hellfire."

I was about to answer with a choice string of curses, when my phone rang. It took me a few seconds to process the number as I put it on speakerphone.

"Shit," I whispered when I realized who the number belonged to. "This is not good."

"Who is it?" Monty asked, looking at the number, and then he shook his head. "It's for you."

It was Ken.

"*Ohayo gozaimasu*, isn't it a little late for you to be up—sun being out and all?" I said as I swerved around traffic.

"Cut the shit, Simon," Ken said with an unnatural

calm, which scared me more than his usual irritation. "We need to meet."

"Sorry, did you mean meet with me in the same physical space?" I answered, trying to deflect what I knew was coming. "Aren't you concerned Monty may destroy whatever building we'll be occupying?"

"I know you know about the Blood Hunters and my sister."

So much for keeping him out of the loop. An angry Ken was a homicidal Ken. A vindictive Ken meant no one and nothing was safe. No one touched his sister and walked away unscathed. They didn't walk away—period. This was going to be all sorts of bad.

"Where?" I said after a pause. No sense in denying it.

"Neutral ground," he said quietly. "The butcher shop you recently redecorated."

"That wasn't us," I corrected. "Beck wanted to show Monty how powerful he was and it blew up in his face—literally."

No answer, except quiet breathing. For him to suggest neutral ground meant we had skated past 'this is a bad situation' into 'we're fucked' territory. I saw Monty clench his jaw and nod as I took another breath.

"When?" I said after a few seconds.

"Now. Bring your mage," Ken said before hanging up.

TWENTY-THREE

THE RANDY RUMP butcher shop-restaurant was owned and operated by a werebear named Jimmy the Cleaver. The last time we were in his shop, we had a conversation with a Negomancer named Beck. He attacked us—in violation of neutral ground protocols—causing massive destruction of the storefront.

The Dark Council had since repaired and renovated The Randy Rump along with its runic defenses. According to Monty, a magic-user attempting to cast inside of its walls now would be rendered unconscious immediately and lose their ability to cast for twenty-four hours. Something about Ziller's metaphysical law of runic backlash. I never paid attention when Monty started with his magicscience explanations. The last time I tried, I had a migraine that lasted three days.

I parked the Goat outside of the Rump next to a blood-red Ecosse Spirit crotch-rocket that belonged to Ken. The street was deserted. For an early morning, there was a disturbing lack of activity. There were no cars or pedestrian traffic to be seen anywhere.

"You think Jimmy cordoned off the Rump?" I asked as I looked into the empty shop. "I have a bad feeling about this."

"Really?" Monty said with a sigh as he stepped out of the car. "Let's go see what he wants."

"I could've said I feel like a redshirt being told to check out that ridge in the distance, but I refrained," I said, joining Monty in front of the Rump.

"Your restraint is astounding," Monty answered as he opened the door. "I don't know how you manage."

We walked in, and behind the counter stood a large man with long gray hair pulled back in a ponytail. He wore an apron over a T-shirt and jeans. His massive arms, which were easily the size of my legs, were covered with thick hair. His mouth was set in a tight line as he cleaned some glasses. He gave me a short nod and pointed to the back corner. The door to the back room was sealed and I breathed a little easier. If Ken had wanted to meet in there, it meant one of us wasn't walking out.

"Did you invoke a cordon?" I asked as I walked up to the counter and took in the shop. Only one person sat at a back table. "It's pretty empty in here."

"I didn't," Jimmy said, looking over his shoulder. "He did. Says he has to give you something and shut down the area. Mentioned Blood Hunters."

A cordon shutdown an area of a square block around a neutral location was usually reserved for high-level meetings between warring factions or powerful enemies. The Dark Council tried to avoid them when they could, due to the area of effect they produced.

It was similar to what Nick did with his plane-weaving but without actually moving the block. Mass disorientation and insane amounts of snarled traffic were always the result of a cordon. If the Dark Council allowed Ken to invoke this one, they were aware of the situation with Michiko.

I took a seat opposite Ken. He wore the usual black-on-black ensemble, a black trench coat over black jeans topped by a black turtleneck sweater. His long hair, hands, neck, and face were covered with a lightweight UV sensitive polymer that hardened when exposed to sunlight.

It allowed vampires to roam the streets during the day without the risk of catching a fatal tan. I called them vajamas, a cross between stylish armor and vampire long-johns. Neither Chi nor Ken approved of my name for their armor. Occasionally, creative genius must go unrecognized.

On the floor next to Ken sat a long narrow case. It matched the smaller one sitting on the table between us. He pressed the side of his neck and a section of the vampire armor receded from his face.

"Strong, mage," Ken said, grabbing the larger case and placing it carefully on the table. "I need you to get my sister back."

"Why isn't the Dark Council doing something about this?" I asked, pointing at him and raising my voice. "She's the leader and they're just going to do what—let the Blood Hunters kill her?"

"Yes," he said quietly. "In order to understand the Council, you must understand supernaturals."

"Rule of strength and power governs the

supernatural community," Monty replied after a pause. "She wasn't voted in. She fought her way to the leadership position."

Ken nodded. "Any sign of weakness and her position can be contested." He opened the large case on the table and I saw the katana Ken usually wore across his back. Its black blade glistened in the low light, threatening to cut me just for looking at it. "She leads the Council because they fear her. Now her enemies see an opportunity."

"*Kokutan no ken*?" I said, admiring the faintly glowing runes along its blade. I'd never seen it unsheathed. A few of the runes matched the ones on Ebonsoul. "This is the dark blade, but they said blades."

"This is one of them, the other is *kokutan no tamashi*," Ken said, looking at me. "The blade you are bonded to."

"Wait, what?" I said, pushing my chair back. "What do you mean bonded?"

"I've never used this blade as a weapon," Ken said, closing the case and pushing it closer to me. "My sister gave it to me to safeguard. I'm only its keeper. You, on the other hand—I have seen you use and be used by your blade."

"You *can't* bond with it, can you?" Monty asked, rubbing his chin. "You would be undone."

Ken shook his head. "Perceptive, mage," Ken said and pulled out a sheet of paper from his coat. "No supernatural can bond with these blades. It would negate their existence if they tried. They were created to destroy us."

Monty narrowed his eyes at me. "Your curse makes

you an aberrant, but not supernatural," Monty said, looking at me and then turning back to Ken. "How did your sister know to give Simon this blade?"

"I don't know how, but she knew he could wield and bond to it," Ken said, placing the paper on the table in front of us. "This leads to the next problem. You can't break his bond."

"It can't be that hard," I said. "Monty can do one of his spells and dissolve the bond. Right?"

Ken pushed the paper forward and Monty picked it up. He held it for a few seconds before making a quick gesture. Runes floated in the air and Monty nodded as they disappeared seconds later.

"I thought no magic could be cast in the Rump?" I said, looking at Monty and expecting some runic hammer to smash him.

"Battle magic is prohibited within these walls," Monty said, still studying the paper. "I just used a quick permutation spell. It has a low probability of activating the runic defense."

"What do you think, mage?" Ken said after a moment. "It only points to one way."

Monty pointed at the paper. "Where did you get this?" I noticed the intricate diagrams surrounded by runes and lines. Concentric circles were intersected by other symbols and surrounded by more runes. "This is a description of Ziller's Quantum Phasic Entanglement, although I've never seen it expressed in quite that manner."

"I'm told that is the bonding process of the blades," Ken answered. "It was given to me by—a—...friend. Do you see the problem?"

"Indeed," Monty muttered, turning the paper over. "The equations are correct. There is only one way to break the bond."

"I knew there was a solution," I said, relieved. "How do we break the bond? What spell? The sooner we do this the sooner we can get Chi."

"No spell is required." Monty reviewed the sheet again. "According to this, it's quite simple. In order to dissolve the bond, the bearer must expire."

"Excuse me?"

"The only way to break the bond is for you to die," Ken said. "Do you see the problem now?"

TWENTY-FOUR

"THERE HAS TO be another way," I said, grabbing the paper from Monty and looking at the indecipherable diagrams. He stared at me with a 'what are you doing?' look. "Maybe you didn't examine the equations correctly?"

Monty extended a hand and I gave the sheet back to him. He reviewed it once more before returning it to Ken. "The equations are sound," Monty said with a nod. "We need alternatives. Do you know where they're holding your sister?"

"No, but I know it has to do with this," Ken said, removing a pouch from the small case. He placed the pouch on the table and opened it. It was another keepsaker box. "I liberated this from a group of Blood Hunters I retired last night. Whoever is flooding the streets with vampire blood is using these boxes to move it."

"What does Redrum have to do with your sister?" I asked, not seeing the connection. "What does that have to do with the blades?"

"The Council—my sister—shut down blood harvesting in this city years ago," Ken said, picking up the keepsaker. "It made her some powerful enemies."

"Enemies who wouldn't mind if she disappeared," Monty said. "Especially if it meant the return of Redrum profits."

"Someone promised the Blood Hunters the dark blades," Ken answered and stood. He pulled another, larger, pouch from the case and handed it to me. "Take this."

"In exchange for removing Michiko from the board," I said, taking the pouch. "They told them to trade Michiko for the blades and then what?"

"What do you think, Simon?" Ken said, pressing the side of his neck, activating a visor across his eyes. "They kill her. What's left of her will be found on a rooftop at sunrise somewhere or they will starve her and cut her loose to be killed by the NYTF or the Council as she rampages."

"Fuck," I said under my breath, examining the pouch he gave me. "What's this?"

"Battle armor for Michiko," Ken said and tapped at the armor on his neck. "Day or night, make sure she puts it on when you find her. It will be the only thing to protect her against blood arrows."

"We can't give the Blood Hunters the blades," Monty whispered as my phone vibrated. "They would bond to them and eliminate all the vampires in the city."

"The streets would flow with Redrum," I said, putting the pouch containing the battle armor in my coat's inner pocket.

"Someone is using Blood Hunters to harvest vampire blood," Ken said as he headed for the door. I followed him and admired the Ecosse as he pushed it off the sidewalk. "Setup a meeting. You have both blades now. Just make sure they don't get them. Find the person using the Blood Hunters—you find my sister."

"What are you going to do?" I asked. My phone vibrated again and I saw it was Ramirez.

"I have to take my sister's place in the Council until she returns," Ken said. "If I take direct action they can invoke a challenge for her seat."

"Which means?" I asked, silencing my phone.

"They will attempt to remove him forcibly if he's seen to interfere," Monty replied. "You know they will issue the challenge regardless."

"If her seat were vacant, a challenge can be issued immediately," Ken said, jumping on the Ecosse and looking in my direction. "If I take her place they have to wait five days. That's how long you have to find her and bring her back to me. If you fail, I'll remember."

Ken started the motorcycle and sped off as my phone vibrated again. I picked it up on the third ring.

"Simon, hello," Ramirez said calmly. His tone threw me for a second because Ramirez only had three voice settings: yelling, screaming, and make your ears bleed. "I'm sitting here in my office across from one Julien Durant, the sovereign of the Foundry, who is filing a formal complaint against the Montague & Strong Detective Agency for damages to his home. Would you happen to know anything about that?"

"It wasn't us," I said, heading back to the table and

picking up the sword case. I gave Jimmy a quick nod, which he returned as I passed the counter and walked out of the shop. Monty unlocked the Goat and jumped in the passenger side. "At least not entirely."

"Of course it wasn't," Ramirez answered and I could hear him tapping a keyboard in the background. "You'll have to come into my office for a formal statement. Please use our new offices. Will you be able to comply or do I need to have Officer Allen issue a warrant?"

"A warrant?" I said, starting the car. "What the hell, Ramirez?"

"Yes or no?" Ramirez said with an edge. "It would be a good idea if you brought in your associate as well. I would hate to have another body turn up. Can I expect you within the hour?"

Then it made sense. The tone. The mention of Allen and a body turning up. He wanted us to meet him at the Medical Examiner's office in an hour. What I didn't understand was why he was being cryptic.

"Yes, we'll be there," I said and hung up. "We need to go see Allen. Something major is going down and I think Julien is part of it."

TWENTY-FIVE

I DROVE UPTOWN to 520 1st Avenue, which was also the OCME, or Office of the Chief Medical Examiner. I just called it the morgue.

We entered the elevator and headed down to the third sub-basement reserved for supernatural deaths. When the doors opened, five NYTF officers standing guard by the elevator greeted us. We flashed our credentials, courtesy of Ramirez, and walked down to the autopsy room.

The smell of chemicals permeated the space and I had to hold my breath for a few seconds as I adjusted. Fluorescent lights kept the room brightly illuminated. Three stainless steel tables dominated the center of the room. Scales hung at the head of each, reminding me of the old hanging meat scales used in butcher shops. Next to each of the autopsy tables sat trays with silver instruments. On the far wall, a sink ran the length of the room.

A body lay on the center table. At least I thought it

was a body. It had been burned beyond recognition. Ramirez stood next to the table with his arms crossed and a scowl on his face. Two more NYTF officers were on the other side of the room. I looked around, but I didn't see Allen.

"I told you not to go in there," Ramirez whispered as he swiped his face in one motion. He pointed to Monty. "Do you know who this was?"

Monty started to shake his head and then I saw the recognition surface in his eyes. "Bloody hell, Ian," Monty whispered as he stepped close to the table. "What happened to you?"

Ramirez pulled out his small pad. "Ian Macintyre, Arbiter Mage of the Golden Circle," Ramirez read off. "According to the eyewitness, Ian here was executed while performing his duties of apprehending one Tristan Montague, rogue mage of the same sect."

"Eyewitness?" I said a little louder than I intended. "We were on the street alone when—he—Ian attacked us."

"Not according to the eyewitness, a Julien Durant, sovereign of the Foundry," Ramirez said and looked at the two NYTF officers in the room. "Let me have a moment."

The officers each gave a short nod and stepped out of the room, keeping their hands close to their holsters. The door closed behind them with a soft click.

"What the hell is going on, Ramirez?" I asked, suddenly angry. "You know this wasn't us."

Ramirez held up a finger and pressed a small cube he held in his other hand. We were suddenly in a sphere of silence. Monty raised an eyebrow and looked around. He gestured as orange runes trailed from his fingers.

"This is a workable silence spell," Monty said and held out his hand to Ramirez. "May I?"

"That's our latest from Jhon our Q-master," Ramirez said, handing Monty the cube. "He calls it silence, cubed. Knock yourself out, just don't touch the red surface or it collapses the area of silence."

Ramirez turned to face me with clenched fists. For a second, I thought he was going to unleash one at my face.

"Angel?" I said, backing up a step. "We should calm down. And by we, I mean *you*."

"What the royal fuck, Simon!" Ramirez screamed, followed by a string of curses in Spanish. "Do you know how deep in the shit you are—the both of you?"

Monty looked up from the cube. "Julien assassinated Ian and is currently claiming us—specifically me—as the guilty party," Monty replied matter-of-factly. "Due to his status as sovereign of the Foundry and his many connections in the city, this will force the NYTF to view us as criminals and attempt to apprehend and detain us."

Ramirez looked at Monty for a second before turning back to me. "That! Exactly that!" Ramirez yelled, poking me in the chest. "I told you not to go in there without an *army* of backup. Why was this guy after you anyway?"

"Doesn't matter now." I looked at the very crispy Ian. "Julien is this powerful, Monty?"

Monty nodded, handing the cube back to Ramirez. "Julien expects us to escape, which will allow him to unleash Claude under the pretense of assisting the incompetent NYTF," Monty said, narrowing his eyes at Ian. "With Ian's death, the Sanctuary will move to the next phase of apprehending me."

"Which is?" I asked, not wanting to hear the answer. "I think we've moved past a strongly worded email."

"They'll send a magistrate," Monty said, his voice grim. "Someone stronger than Ian."

"That sounds bad," I said. "How bad is it?"

"Within the Golden Circle, magistrates are only second to the elders in power," Monty replied. "He won't be here to escort me back. Not after what happened to Ian—and he won't be alone."

"So magistrates are basically Golden Circle assassins," I said, looking at the charred remains of Ian. "Are they stronger than you?"

Monty gave me a short nod. "Considerably older and stronger," Monty answered, stepping away from what used to be Ian. "Julien will accomplish his goal of eliminating us without having to leave the Foundry. If that fails, he has considerable resources at his disposal. I'm sure this moved quickly through the NYTF brass."

Ramirez nodded. "I can give you two hours before the order goes out and NYTF mobilizes to bring you in," Ramirez replied. "I brought you here because I don't know who I can trust right now and we needed to meet face-to-face. You need to make it look real."

"Make what look real?" I said, confused. "What are you talking about?"

"Our escape," Monty said and formed an orb of air in his hand. "Are you ready, Director?"

"Those guys outside are good guys," Ramirez said,

bracing himself. "Rough them up, but nothing permanent? Deal?"

Monty nodded. "You have my word." Monty gestured and the orb in his hand picked up speed. "Please stand by the wall; it will lessen the impact."

Ramirez held up a hand signaling Monty to wait.

"One more thing and the real reason I needed you on this," Ramirez said as he stood by the wall. "The Redrum flooding the streets is being controlled by someone who calls himself the Wraith. One of my sources says he's a mage working with someone inside the Dark Council. If this information is solid, this is about more than just Redrum."

"Are you kidding me?" I said, slamming a table with my fist and looking at Monty. "Fucking Nick? I told you we should have erased him."

"We may well get the chance," Monty said, and let go of the orb in his hand. "Brace yourself, Director."

"Find this Wraith and stop him before every street in the city runs red with vampire blood," Ramirez said right before the orb bounced him off the wall. I caught him and laid his unconscious form on the floor.

"I think he's on Peaches' pastrami diet," I said with a grunt as I moved him, taking care not to bump his head against the floor. "Seven officers outside. My methods are lethal. I hope you have something gentler than Ebonsoul or entropy rounds."

"I do, but I'm going to need your shield," Monty said with a gesture.

I opened the door and pressed the main bead on my mala bracelet. A shield materialized in front of me. Monty placed a hand on the shield and muttered some words under his breath. It contorted and changed shape. A cylinder of white energy blasted down the hallway, slamming the officers against the walls.

"You call that gentle?" I said as we walked to the elevator. A few of the officers groaned in pain. Some of them were out cold as we stepped by them.

"They're still alive and our escape needed to appear authentic," Monty answered, entering the elevator. "I've achieved both and left them mostly intact."

I just stared at him as the elevator doors closed. We exited the building and jumped into the Goat. Monty grabbed a mage powerbar, closed his eyes, and rested his head back against the seat.

"You good?" I asked, concerned. He was looking a little pale. "Is it tea time?"

He nodded but kept his eyes closed as I started the car. "I need to go to the office," he said, opening his eyes and taking another bite of the bar. "These bars, aside from tasting like dirt, are not helping much. I need something stronger."

TWENTY-SIX

I PULLED UP in front of the Moscow. I grabbed the sword case, locked the car, and left the Goat in front of the building. I didn't expect us to stay long and explained as much to the valet, who headed back to the garage.

Andrei opened the door and looked around me nervously. "Where is *ad soba*—your big dog?"

I gave him points for the quick recovery.

"Peaches, his name is Peaches, and he's at the doctor, not feeling well," I said, entering the lobby. "We'll be down in ten minutes."

Andrei let out an audible sigh of relief and smiled. "What happened?" Andrei asked, chuckling. "Dog eat car?"

"Hilarious, Andrei, I'll make sure to let him play with you when he gets out," I said, heading for the stairs. "I'm sure he'd love a new chew toy."

Andrei shook his head and held his hands up in mock surrender, before crossing himself, suddenly serious. "*Nyet, net spasibo.* No thank you."

Monty shook his head as we headed for the stairwell. "You need to stop torturing the man," he said, opening the door.

"I live for the small pleasures." I climbed the stairs with Monty behind me. "Besides, he started it."

I needed to call Roxanne and see how Peaches was doing. With everything that was going on, I hadn't had a chance to check up on him. Peaches technically *was* a helldog, but he was *my* helldog. Which meant no one else got to call him that.

I was about to pull out my phone as we reached our floor, when I noticed the door to the office was wide open. Monty stepped up behind me and cursed under his breath.

Thanks to Olga, the prestigious law firm of Christye, Blahq, & Doil were graciously relinquishing another small corner of the floor space we shared. It allowed us to add another three rooms to our office. The new space was being converted into more living quarters, an expansion to the office space, a larger reception area, and a meditation room for Monty. I think they had been using the space as a storage closet.

A few days back I had stopped and knocked on their door to express my thanks at their generosity and, of course, the office was closed. The agreement meant we were going to be renovating soon, but there was no scheduled work today. I drew Grim Whisper as Monty gestured next to me.

"They bypassed the runic defenses but left them intact," Monty whispered, forming an orb of blue energy in his hand. "Whoever did this is an accomplished mage, beyond my ability."

"Julien?" I whispered, standing next to the door with my gun in a high ready position. "Can he do this?"

"Julien prefers to act from the shadows." Monty shook his head slowly. "Much less come here and infiltrate our home, which would be beneath him. He has Claude for that, but Claude is incapable of wielding magic at this level."

That's when the smell hit me. The aroma of sausage, eggs, and coffee wafted out of the office, filled my lungs and nestled, reminding me I had skipped breakfast.

"Whoever it is decided to make us breakfast before attacking," I whispered, trying to keep from drooling. "I say we sit down, have a meal, before we engage in the violence."

"This is serious, Simon," Monty said, increasing the size of the orb from a grapefruit to a basketball of destruction. "Weaving magic at this level requires an immense amount of skill and energy. If the runic defenses have been circumvented without detonation it means we are facing a major threat."

"Well, that major threat is killing me with this smell and I skipped breakfast, so throw your basketball of pain and let's get this over with," I said over the rumbling in my stomach.

"It's not a basketball of pain, it's called a runic magical disruptor and should allow us to—never mind," Monty said when he saw my expression.

"I don't need the magicscience." I pointed at the door. "I need breakfast."

Monty released the orb of energy and it raced inside

the office. A few seconds later, a blue flash nearly blinded me as the orb bounced back into the hallway where we stood, and detonated. Monty threw up a shield and deflected the wave of energy away from us.

"If you're done playing with your magical balls, Tristan, I'd suggest coming in and having breakfast," a voice with Monty's accent called out from inside. "Nice rune work, by the way."

"Someone you know?" I said, looking at Monty's surprised expression. I was still blinking the spots out of my eyes.

"Impossible," whispered Monty as he entered the office.

I stepped in slowly, cutting the corner and saw a naked man sitting in our dining area, having breakfast. His upper body was a mosaic of scars. As I looked closer, I realized that the scars were really runes etched into his skin. Two lines of text surrounded by more runes were tattooed on each of his forearms. My Latin was rusty but I still remembered enough to decipher his ink. One read *dum spiro spero*, while I breathe, I hope. On the other it read *deponite omnes spes,* abandon all hope.

Perched behind him had to be the largest raven in existence. It sat on a long thick gnarled branch that leaned against a wall, with its eyes closed. I had seen that branch somewhere but couldn't place it. I holstered Grim Whisper and placed the sword case on the table.

"Who are you?" I racked my brain, trying to place his face. "I've seen you before. How long did it take to get the rune work done?"

He narrowed his eyes at me.

"You have, have you?" Naked Man answered around a forkful of food. "That's quite impressive, since my veil is one of the best." He waved a hand and I recognized him instantly. It was the homeless man from the street. The one who was sleeping on the sidewalk when we fought Ian. "And you can see my runes?"

"You?" I nodded in recognition. "What are you doing here? Who *are* you?"

"Tristan hasn't mentioned me?" the man said and looked at Monty with a huge grin on his face. "I'm offended, nephew. Cut to the quick, even."

"You're sitting in our home, bloody naked, and you're wondering why I haven't mentioned you?" Monty said and stormed off. "Wait right there."

"Nephew?" I asked, confused. "You're his uncle?"

The old man nodded at me with a wicked smile. He motioned for me to sit down and eat. The table was covered with a wonderful spread of food. Some of the food I recognized, other plates were a mystery. I grabbed a plate and filled it with everything. My phone vibrated a few seconds later. It was Roxanne.

"Simon, I'm so sorry," she said, crying as she spoke. "He's gone. Peaches is gone."

My heart stopped and my stomach clenched at her words. I took a deep breath and then another. "Explain it to me slowly, Roxanne," I said calmly. "What happened exactly?"

"He was recovering and had regained consciousness," she started as the words tumbled out. "We had him strapped down to administer another dose of antitoxin when he just—he just vanished."

I smiled and my heart started beating again. I let out the breath I had been holding. "I'm the one that should be sorry, Roxanne," I said. "He has a tendency to do that."

"He *what*?" Roxanne recovered with an edge in her voice. "And you didn't think mentioning a disappearing hellhound was relevant? I thought we killed him, Simon."

"He's pretty indestructible," I said when I heard the familiar growl. "I think I just found him."

"Thank goodness," Roxanne said and let out a long breath. "I swear, between you and Tristan…Please bring in your *dog* when you can. I still need to run some tests and make sure the neurotoxin is out of his system. Oh and please express my thanks to Tristan for the new MRI scanner."

I turned to see Peaches stalking Monty's uncle. He was in 'pounce and shred' mode and this looked like it was going to be ugly. The raven sitting on the branch opened its eyes and they flared a bright green. It spread its wings, which covered most of the wall with its wingspan. Monty's uncle was focused on the slowly approaching dog of destruction. He gestured slowly as he turned his body to face Peaches.

"I will," I said quickly. "Have to go."

Monty's uncle raised a hand, still focused on Peaches. A large sausage materialized in his palm. He offered the sausage to Peaches slowly. The raven pulled its wings tight but kept its glowing eyes on Peaches.

Peaches closed in on the outstretched hand and removed the sausage, as I looked on, stunned. He brought the sausage next to me and proceeded to devour it.

"It's good to see the security of our home is such a priority to you." I looked down at him as he chomped on the sausage in delight.

<He smells like the angry one. I'm hungry. Do you see this meat? It's good.>

"You almost gave Roxanne a heart attack," I said, crouching down and rubbing his neck. "She thought you were dead when you vanished on her."

<She was going to poke me with one of those metal sticks. They hurt, so I left, and I was hungry.>

"How did you find me?" I asked, curious.

<Find you? I always know where you are.>

I looked up and caught Monty's uncle staring at us.

"You're bonded to one of Cerberus' pups?" he said, the surprise clear in his voice. "I've only seen that twice before in my lifetime. Hades must hold you in high regard. What's his name?"

"Peaches," I said, expecting some comment.

Monty's uncle slapped the table as he burst out in laughter. "That Hades has a twisted sense of humor—Peaches! Ha!" he managed once he caught his breath. He narrowed his eyes and examined Peaches. "That name is perfect for your pup."

"I think Hades just didn't know what to do with him and wanted to torture me," I said, standing and extending my hand. "I'm Simon, and you are?"

"I'm the uncle no one mentions," he said with a sly grin. "The name is Dexter, but everyone calls me Dex. Tristan really hasn't mentioned me?"

"No, not really," I said, shaking my head. "I just

recently heard about William. Until now I thought Monty was an only child."

Dex's face darkened at the mention of William. "He may as well be one, with him for a brother," Dex muttered with a shake of his head. "That one is black inside. No matter what we tried, he went dark."

Monty came back into the dining area with a neat pile of black clothes in his arms. "These should fit," Monty said tersely. "Please get dressed and make yourself presentable."

Dex finished eating, took the clothes, and headed out of dining area with a whistle. "I'll be right back, please enjoy the breakfast," Dex said, shaking his ass and dancing what could only be described as a sloppy jig.

"I really didn't need that visual," I said, looking away. "Why is he here?"

"No one determines where my uncle goes or when," Monty answered with a sigh. "My family has officially disowned him. The Sanctuary elders gave up on him long ago, mostly because he's stronger than most of them."

"Really? But he looks so, I don't know—" I started.

"Deranged is the word you're looking for," Monty said, pouring himself some tea. "May as well eat. He *is* a fantastic cook."

Dexter returned dressed in a slate gray suit over a crisp white shirt. A deep indigo tie accented the ensemble. I saw the resemblance immediately. Where Monty was tall and thin, Dex was a little shorter and rounded out. His salt-and-pepper hair was long like Monty's, but the face gave it away. Dex was an older

Blood Is Thicker

Monty with laugh lines. Something I was sure Monty would never suffer from.

Monty shook his head. "Uncle Dex, the clothes I gave you were black," Monty said with a sigh. "Why did you change them?"

Dex held up two fingers as he walked over to where Peaches was still wrestling with the sausage. "Two things: I'm not headed to a bloody funeral, and everyone needs a little color in their life—that isn't black," Dex said, rubbing the back of Peaches' neck and surprisingly kept his hand attached to the rest of his body. He gave me a quick glance. "How long since you've bonded to the pup?"

"Not long, a few months," I said, still in shock that Peaches let him manhandle him while he ate. "May I ask you a question, Dex?"

"Of course. Any friend of Tristan's has a friend in me." Dex nodded and glanced at Monty with a smile. "You want to know what we called Tristan as a boy?"

"You mentioned you've seen two others bonded to dogs like Peaches," I said, shaking my head even though the temptation was strong. "Have you ever seen that bond broken?"

Dex became serious as he glanced off into the distance. "Together you and this pup will be a force of nature," Dex murmured. "These dogs only bond once in their lives. If that bond is broken in any way, it's best they are put down before they turn."

"Turn?" I asked, suddenly concerned. "Into what?"

"This isn't a real dog, young man, even if it loosely resembles one." Dex fixed his dark eyes on me and stood. "This is the offspring of a monster. Only your bond keeps that part of him in check. You break that bond and you'll have unleashed a creature that's nearly impossible to kill and capable of wonderful amounts of destruction. That would be a bad idea. Now, which room is mine?"

"Excuse me?" Monty asked, flustered, and nearly spilling his tea. "You're staying? I thought you were passing through? Aren't you just visiting?"

Dex gave Monty a look and smiled. "Do you know why he doesn't mention me?" Dex grabbed a large duffel bag from under the table. "It's because his side of the family is a bit stiff and frowns upon my lifestyle."

"Your *lifestyle* usually puts everyone around you in mortal danger, Uncle Dex," Monty responded with shake of his head. "The last time I saw you, you were summoning a demon from the lower depths because you wanted to test a spell that would make hell freeze over."

"Oh, that." Dex absentmindedly waved Monty's words away. "Didn't work. Too damn hot, but the succubae—oof. I couldn't walk straight for a week. Then Mo gave me that infernal raven. Said I needed protection."

"Mo?" I looked at Monty, who shook his head at me. "Who's Mo?"

"Morrigan, Goddess of War, Chooser of the Slain and all-around pain in my arse," Dex answered with a scowl as he looked over his shoulder at the raven perched on the branch. The raven squawked in response. "It's complicated. Gave me Herk for 'protection.' She says protect, I say spy."

Blood Is Thicker

Monty cleared his throat.

"The summoning wouldn't have been an issue if you didn't perform it in the middle of *Saint Peter's Square*," Monty said, exasperated. "You nearly caused an international incident."

I nearly spit out my coffee. "In the Vatican?" I asked, suppressing laughter. "Did you meet the Pope?"

"Don't encourage him." Monty crossed his arms. "He nearly started another Holy War."

"It was the ideal location," Dex shot back with a grin. "Strong belief is a perfect catalyst for that kind of spell. Did you forget everything I taught you?"

"We do have the extra bedroom," I volunteered, and Monty shot daggers at me with a look. "He could use that."

"Perfect!" Dex slung the bag over his shoulder. "No need to escort, I know my way around. I've been in your lovely home a few hours now. Come, Herkrekkr."

"Did Father send you?" Monty asked, suddenly serious. "Is that why you're here?"

"Now, why would he do that?" Dex asked, turning to face Monty. "It's not like you cast a forbidden spell in a city—twice. Those acts would never cause the Elders of your sect, of which your Father is a ranking member, to send the magical police to collect a reckless mage who endangered the lives of an entire city. No—they would just ignore something like that. Wouldn't you agree?"

"There were extenuating circumstances," Monty muttered, looking away. "It was a matter of life and death."

"Of course it was," Dex said, nodding. "Speaking of

death…The sudden demise of the Arbiter tasked with bringing you back to said Elders will only fill them with goodwill toward you and your friend here. This is why they'll unleash a team of magistrates shortly."

"That's an overreaction on their part." Monty drank some more tea and narrowed his eyes at the raven. "No one was harmed and the city is intact."

"Just like the Foundry." Dex nodded. "You're fortunate the Fleur de Lis didn't send one of their own for the destruction of their fancy property."

"That wasn't us," I said around a mouthful of food. "Julien had a nasty guest."

"That sect was always a bit sensitive." Dex dropped the bag and poured himself some coffee as I stared in surprise. "Their Arch Mage looked like his underwear was squeezing his bollocks," Dex said with a grin.

He made a squeezing motion with his hand, stuck out his tongue, and crossed his eyes. I nearly choked on my food at his expression. Monty gave me a look and then stared at Dex.

"*You* destroyed the concrete slab," Monty said, pointing at Dex. "I knew it was too precise to be Julien."

"I have no idea what you're talking about, Tristan," Dex said, shrugging. "But being crushed by a concrete slab is the least of your worries."

"How soon?" Monty asked, his voice tight. "How soon before they arrive?"

"Doesn't matter," Dex said, sipping his coffee. "You two can't face them. Not even with the pup and a few decades to prepare. Word has it they're giving this over to the Ghosts."

"Bloody hell," Monty said and ran a hand through his hair. "The Elders would never go this far—not for a void vortex. Something is wrong."

"Who are the Ghosts?" I asked. "They sound unpleasant."

"That's one way to describe them," Dex answered. "Ghosts are magistrates trained to be instruments of death—lethal and extremely unpleasant. Can't wait to meet them."

"Uncle Dex, no," Monty said, shaking his head. "You can't do this. It will only make things worse."

Dex laughed. "Tristan, you are buried so deep, the only thing you see when you look up is more dirt," Dex said and grew serious. "You are a Montague and we'll not be hunted down like some wild dog over a rule established centuries ago. Not while I still breathe. I do agree with you on one point—something *is* wrong at the Sanctuary."

"This is a disaster." Monty pinched the bridge of his nose and stood. "This is the equivalent of putting out a fire with gasoline. What was Father thinking?"

"Probably how to keep you alive without going against all of the Elders," I said, digging in to more food.

"If it's any solace, Mo suggested I visit you as well."

"Did she say why?" Monty asked. "Or was she her usual forthcoming self?"

Dex shook his head with the hint of a smile. "She only said it was important I was near you, didn't say why," Dex answered. "But you know her, never big on explanations."

"Sounds like a good idea he's here." I finished the

rest of my coffee. "We could use the help, especially if the Golden Circle wants you erased."

The raven took flight and perched on Dex's shoulder as he grabbed the large branch. "I'm only staying a short while." Dex picked up and adjusted the bag on his back. "Until we sort out this mess you've gotten yourself in. It's like you said—I'm just passing through. Oh, and please knock before visiting, I'll be making alterations to my living quarters—wouldn't want either of you shipped off somewhere."

Dex headed down the hallway and disappeared around a corner with a wave.

I looked at Monty, confused. "Alterations?"

"It's better you don't ask," Monty said, heading to the kitchen. "We need to go see Erik."

TWENTY-SEVEN

WE HEADED DOWNSTAIRS and Andrei nearly lost it when he saw Peaches. I smiled and Monty shook his head, walking ahead of us.

"Why don't you go over and say hello, boy?" I said loudly enough for Andrei to hear. "Andrei missed you."

<*Can I bite him? I'm not hungry, but I can chew on him a bit.*>

"No, don't bite him, just growl when you walk next to him," I whispered as we approached the exit. "He'll love that."

Peaches started a rumble low in his chest. It hit jackhammer level when we got to the door. He bared his fangs in some semblance of a smile. Except that dogs, lacking lips, don't have the capacity to smile. It appeared that Peaches was going to snack on Andrei, who stumbled back a few feet.

"*Bozhe moi!*" Andrei said and made sure the door was between him and Peaches. "My God, keep dog away, Stronk."

Peaches just kept walking out to the car and waited. I opened the back door to the Goat and let him jump in. The car rocked from side to side as he settled into the backseat and sprawled. I placed the sword case on the floor next to him and turned to give Andrei a wave before getting behind the wheel and pulling away.

"You're going to have to stop terrorizing him before Olga decides to *ban* your dog from the building," Monty said, looking at the keepsaker. "A petrified doorman is poor security."

"You have a point," I said as I jumped on the Westside Highway and headed to the Hellfire. "Do you think Erik is going to help us? We didn't exactly leave on the best of terms last time I was there."

"You mean *you* didn't leave on the best of terms," Monty replied, touching different sides of the box. "He and I have no issues. Besides, we won't be using the gates today."

"We won't?" I said, surprised, and swerved around a taxicab, one of our city's finest yellow kamikazes. "I thought everyone used the gates—no exceptions?"

"I'm not seeking entrance into the club," Monty said, pulling out his phone. "I need to speak to Erik personally."

"The last time I needed to speak to him personally, I had to go through the gates," I said, taking the exit that would lead us to City Hall.

"*You* aren't capable of reducing his club to rubble, although you did set off all of his defenses," Monty said, and almost smiled.

"That wasn't me," I countered. "That was your psycho mage friend, Quan."

"Whom you pissed off." Monty gestured quickly. A small violet orb floated in front of him. "It's possible Erik just doesn't like you."

"Technically she was pissed off at *you* and set off all of the defenses." I glanced at the bright orb. "What's that?"

"*This* is how we get Erik's attention." Monty let the orb float out of the window. "Take us to the main entrance."

It was early afternoon and traffic was light as we approached the rear of the building. I parked the car near the kiosk I'd used last time. I locked the Goat with the usual clang and orange flare of runes across its surface.

In front of the kiosk stood a woman dressed in a skintight, black-and-white checkered costume. Her face was hidden behind a black mask. The mask was a combination of tragedy and comedy. She bowed with a flourish and twirled the pair of rune-covered tonfas she held when I approached. This was one of the Harlequins—protectors of the Hellfire.

She stood to one side of the large, rune-inscribed circle that rested at the top of the stairs. In order to get into the Hellfire you needed to step in that circle—no exceptions. We stepped in. I adjusted the sword case, and prepared for digestive torture.

"He's expecting me," Monty said with a bow, pointing to Peaches and me. "They are with me."

The Harlequin returned the bow and slammed both tonfas into the ground. The circle we stood in flared to life. A second later, we stood at the foot of a flight of stairs that led to a large wooden door. The next second, the nausea gripped me, and my breakfast threatened to eject itself. I hated teleportation. It always had the effect of twisting my insides out. Monty and Peaches, however, looked unbothered.

I leaned against a wall and recovered. At the top of the stairs stood three Harlequins. Two of them bookended the door. The third stood directly in front of it. Monty bowed to the Harlequin in the center. She returned the bow and waved a hand in the air.

"Welcome, Mage Montague," she said with a flourish. "He is expecting you."

The Harlequins weren't window-dressing. According to Monty, they were handpicked and trained by Erik into an elite security force. Each of them was an accomplished mage and could wield their runed tonfas with deadly efficiency. In other words, if you followed the rules, you left Hellfire alive; if you broke them, they broke you.

The large wooden door opened into Erik's office. I stood there dumbfounded and a little angry, remembering the gates I had to pass the last time I was here.

Erik sat in an oversized chair behind his large desk and waited as we entered. A Harlequin closed the door behind us. Two more Harlequins bookended his desk. The office, though large, felt inviting. Bookshelves filled with books covered every wall. I looked around, noticing that the collection and the shelf space had grown.

"Don't piss him off—yet," Monty whispered as we approached the two large wingback chairs facing the desk. Peaches padded silently next to me. "He can help us find your vampire."

Erik looked up from a pile of papers and gave us a tight smile. He was dressed in a dark suit, which mages seemed to favor, with a crisp white shirt and no tie. He waved a hand and the Harlequins left the room silently.

"This isn't a good time, Tristan, as I'm sure you're aware," Erik said once the Harlequins were gone. "Please, sit."

"Do you know where she is?" I asked, refusing to sit in the wingback. I heard Monty sigh next to me as he sat down.

"And hello to you too, Simon," Erik replied, sitting back in his chair. "Your decorum never ceases to amaze."

"Answer the question," I said, clenching a fist. Peaches rumbled next to me, sensing my agitation. "Do you?"

"Of course I know where she is," Erik said and threw his hands up. I flinched and my hand reflexively moved to rest on Grim Whisper. Mages and gestures are a dangerous combination. "Getting to her is another matter entirely."

TWENTY-EIGHT

"WE NEED HER location," Monty said quietly as he reached in a pocket and pulled out the keepsaker. He placed it on the desk and pushed it forward. "The Blood Hunters are using these to store the blood they harvest."

"No." Erik reached over and picked up the keepsaker. "This one"—he pointed at me—"will try to rescue her and get everyone killed in the process," Erik said, turning the box. "The Blood Hunters are not a small group of psychopaths, they are an army of psychopaths with one driving purpose: the elimination of vampires. You don't reason with them, you don't appeal to their sense of right and wrong. They are relentlessly driven to achieve one goal. Nothing can stop them except their own annihilation. I don't care how immortal you think you are"—Erik pointed at me again—"or how powerful you may be after your shift, Tristan. Neither of you is immune to the explosive properties of their blood arrows."

"I need you to set up a meet with their leader, Erik," I said in an even tone, surprising myself, and apparently Monty who glanced over at me. "I need to meet with Anastasia."

Erik placed the box on the desk and shot me a look. "How did you get that name?" he asked, steepling his fingers and leaning back in his chair. "Who have you spoken to?"

"We met with her second, Esti, at the Foundry," Monty answered. "We didn't get to finish the conversation."

"It was you two at the Foundry, I should've known. No wonder Julien is livid."

"Esti and her knives are partly to blame for that," I added quickly. "She tried to convince us to hand over the dark blades."

"And yet you're still breathing? Amazing." Erik shifted some papers around. "She is the most dangerous of the Blood Hunters. If she led them, we would be at war right now."

"We have something they want." I tapped the case. "They have someone we want. It's a simple exchange."

"You don't get it, Simon," Erik said, pulling up a sheet. "Michiko is as good as dead. They aren't going to *trade* with you. They will take the blades, find a way to kill all of you and then systematically cleanse the city of vampires."

"We need your help," I said after a pause. "Just tell me where they are and set up the meet."

"I'm on the Council," Erik said, standing. "Do you know what you're asking?"

"I know the Council won't act, in fact some of them

want her out of the way, but you aren't one of them," I answered and looked him in the eyes. "You aren't her enemy and you understand the shitstorm that's coming if they remove her. Just tell me where she is and we'll take it from there."

Erik walked over to one of the bookcases. "Shit," he muttered, looking at Monty. "Is he always this difficult?"

"Only when he's awake," Monty said and nodded sagely. "Can you do it?"

"I'm going to need that," Erik said, pointing at the case holding the katana. "Anastasia won't agree otherwise."

Monty rubbed his chin. "How long will it take to set up the meet?" he asked, looking at the case. "I need to take some precautions."

"A few hours," Erik answered. "She isn't exactly the trusting type. They will want to see and test the blade before meeting."

"That should give me enough time," Monty said, taking the case from my hands. "In the meantime, I need to go to the Sanctuary."

"It's clear that your exposure to Simon has addled your senses," Erik said, shaking his head. "Enjoy your trip. Give my regards to the Elders—who, if my sources are correct, want you dead."

"I need the Hellfire as an anchor," Monty said, looking at Erik. "I need you to open a portal there."

Erik let out a deep breath. "You want me to open a portal to the Sanctuary?" Erik raised his voice and pointed at Monty. I felt the energy in the room increase. He was getting agitated, which was always a bad thing for a mage. "Do you really think I'm suicidal? Fuck no, Tristan. The moment I do, they'll assume I had something to do with a certain dead Arbiter. How dare you come in here demanding—?"

"I'm not demanding," Monty replied quietly. "I'm asking as a friend."

"You don't know what you're asking." Erik sat down at his desk again. He poured himself a small glass of the clear liquid he kept in a decanter on his desk. "This is worse than asking where Michiko is."

"I wouldn't think of imposing on you this way, but they're sending the Ghosts." Monty let the words hang in the air. "I need to know why they would go that far."

Erik poured himself another glass of the liquid. "Shit, Tristan, just go home," Erik whispered. "Face them and resolve this."

"No," Monty said, his voice steel. "Now *you* don't know what you're asking. This is the only way."

Erik closed his eyes, rubbed his face, and let out a sigh. "How many are traveling?" Erik said, making a gesture. Red trails followed his fingers. "I'm going to have to bring in a specialist."

"Three: Simon, his creature, and myself," Monty said, standing. "Aria would be perfect for this."

"Thought this all out, have you?" Erik answered and scowled. "Of course she would be perfect for this, she's a bloody Smith. I hate your scheming, manipulative, arrogant ass right now, Tristan."

"I'm in your debt," Monty said, and then he gestured. A golden orb floated from his fingers and landed on the desk, disappearing as it did. "If you ever need my assistance, call me."

"Tristan, *that* wasn't necessary," Erik whispered, shaking his head. "But thank you. The workshop is available for your *precautions*. I'll let you know when Aria and the portal are ready."

"What was that?" I asked as we left Erik's office, escorted by Harlequins. "The gold orb? I've never seen that."

The Harlequins led us down several corridors. We bypassed the dungeons and so avoided the acts of consensual erotic torture. We came to a small empty rune-covered room filled with worktables. One side of the room held beakers and liquids while the other was filled with worn books. It reminded me of every science classroom I sat in during high school.

Monty placed the sword case on one of the tables and opened it, revealing the katana—*kokutan no ken*. The black blade shimmered in the bright light of the workshop. Monty narrowed his eyes for a few seconds before looking up and shifting his gaze to one of the Harlequins.

"I'm going to need a sword similar to this one, with a matching case," Monty said to the Harlequin. "I'm sure Erik has one in his armory."

They bowed and silently stepped out of the room. Monty took off his jacket and rolled up his sleeves. He removed the sword from the case and placed it on the table.

"The orb you saw is called an invoker," Monty said, gesturing over the blade.

"And it does…?" I asked, staying on the blunt side of the incredibly sharp sword. "And why do you need another sword?"

"If Erik ever needs my help, he can use it to summon me from wherever I may be," Monty said as he placed his hands on the hilt.

"Like a genie?" I asked, feeling the increase of runic energy build up around the room. I noticed the door was locked—from the outside. "What if you're in the bathroom? Or with Roxanne?"

"It requires my consent," Monty said, giving me a 'don't be dense' look. "I'm not some demon to be summoned into a circle. That being said, it's poor form to refuse an invocation once summoned."

The door to the workshop opened and a Harlequin entered, holding another case. She placed it on the table, bowed again, and left. I heard the locks securing the door.

"Why are they locking the door?" I asked, looking around. "It's not like we're trying to escape."

"Anytime this workshop is in use, that door is locked, especially when a high level spell is being performed," Monty answered and removed the second sword from its case. It looked identical to *kokutan no ken* except this black blade was naked of runes.

"Do I really need to be in here?" I asked, acutely aware of the size the room. The lack of cover provided by the thin tables heightened my feelings of exposure. "I could always scrounge up some food for Peaches."

<*I could eat.*>

"When couldn't you?" I said, looking down at him. "He definitely agrees with my plan of finding food—outside of this room."

Monty placed the two swords side by side. "They won't unlock the door until I finish." Monty adjusted the blades so they were exactly next to each other. "This isn't a transmutative spell. The potential for mishap is great if you don't let me concentrate."

"That's great, but it would help if I understood the words coming out of your mouth." I began arranging the tables to provide some kind of cover. "If it's not a mutation then what is it?"

"*Transmutation*," Monty answered, still focused on the blades. "It means I can't make an exact copy of this dark blade. It's too old and imbued with too much power. I'm creating a fake that has its most important property. If I get this wrong, they'll be sponging us up from the floor."

"Now I'm all encouraged," I said, moving as far away as possible from him. "Didn't Erik say they were going to test it too?"

Monty nodded and began gesturing again. "I'm going to duplicate the runes I can decipher," he said and held out his hand. "For the rest I'm going to need your blade and blood."

"My *blood*?" I unsheathed Ebonsoul and approached him. "How much blood are we talking here?"

"A few drops should suffice." Monty pointed at the new blade. "Here, rub the blood on this blade."

I pricked my finger with Ebonsoul and let the drops fall on the blade. Monty moved his hand over the sword and the blood disappeared, absorbed into the blade.

"And we need my blood because…?" I looked closely at the blade as it began to change, becoming darker.

"Transmuting this sword is beyond me." He pointed

at the *kokutan no ken*. "What I'm doing is creating a copy that will exhibit the properties of the original. Your blood—more importantly, your magical immunity—can be adjusted to nullify magic for a short time…if I do this right."

"And if you do it wrong?" I stepped from behind the worktable holding the blades. "Were you serious about being sponged off the floor?"

He gave me a look and went back to muttering words under his breath. I recognized the expression. It was his 'keep talking and get us killed' look. I shut up and went back to my makeshift cover of lab tables. I pulled Peaches close and made sure we were as far from the blades and Monty as possible.

<*Is he going to make meat like the birdman?*>

"Birdman?" I realized he meant Dex. "No, he's going to try very hard not to explode us."

<*Can he make more meat? I'm getting hungry.*>

"Once we get out of here, I'll get you some food." I rubbed his neck and kept my hand close to my mark. If I saw things go sideways, at least I could buy us some time.

Monty placed his hands together and closed his eyes. He whispered some words under his breath and I felt the pressure increase as the runes along the walls flared to life. A black swirl of energy formed around him. He opened his eyes and they had gone full mage. Each iris was pitch black with a glowing golden circle around it. He separated his palms and placed them on the fake sword. The black swirl funneled down into the blade with a palpable thump. My ears popped and I felt the energy race across the floor and shake the walls. Monty remained frozen in place for several minutes as the energy flowed out of him and into the blade. When he removed his hands from the table, there were two *kokutan no ken* sitting side by side.

He took the fake and placed it in the original case. The real blade he placed on the floor next to him.

"I need to put this somewhere safe in case this plan fails." Monty traced several runes in the air. They fell to the floor and formed a circle around the blade. In moments, the blade disappeared. He sagged over the table and reached in his pocket, pulling out a large flat brown wafer.

"Where did you send it?" I stepped over the makeshift cover of tables with Peaches in tow. "Are you okay?"

"I'll be fine in a moment." Monty took a bite out of the wafer and the color returned to his face. "It's safe. The Blood Hunters would find it impossible to retrieve."

I was about to ask where exactly he sent it, when the door unlocked and a Harlequin entered.

"Would you kindly give this to Erik for his arrangement?" Monty said as he grabbed the case and handed it to the Harlequin.

"Your portal is ready," she said as she took the case, bowed, and left the room.

I waited until she was gone and turned to Monty. "How long will the copy last?"

"Two days, three at most." Monty finished the remaining half of the wafer. "Depends on how it's tested."

"Two days to find Chi and get her back in one

piece." I rubbed Peaches behind the ears. "We don't even know where they have her."

"Erik knows and he *will* tell us." Monty brushed the crumbs off his shirt and put on his jacket. "In the meantime we'll go see why the Golden Circle is so eager to see me dead."

TWENTY-NINE

THE LAST TIME I visited a pocket dimension I had made a trip to Japan to see Quan. This time we were headed to some unknown location "in the mountains," which was the only information Monty would share when I asked about the location of the Sanctuary.

We entered Erik's office, behind the Harlequin holding the sword case. He placed the case on his desk and opened it.

"Tristan, are you sure this is the copy?" Erik held the sword in his hand. "How did you manage this?"

"Seventy-two hours on the outside and then it reverts." Monty answered, pointing at the case. "The less it's handled the better."

Erik returned the sword with a shake of his head. "Your talents never cease to surprise me," he said, closing the case. "The portal is waiting, as is Aria. I take it you wanted to speak to her?"

"Yes, about this." Monty fished out the keepsaker. "She would know who requested them."

"The Blood Hunters, I would assume," Erik said and sat behind his desk. "I don't suppose I can convince you to cancel this trip to the Sanctuary?"

Monty shook his head. "The Blood Hunters wouldn't have access to the Smiths to make the request, and no, you can't," Monty answered, replacing the box in a pocket. "She may be able to shed some light on who is behind this."

"The anchor will retrieve you in thirty minutes." Erik poured himself another glass of the clear liquid. "I figured that was enough time for you to find out why your sect wants you gone."

"Retrieve us?" I looked from Erik to Monty. "What does he mean?"

"Creating a pocket dimension into the Sanctuary requires an immense amount of energy due to the runic defenses," Monty said, walking over to the door on the other side of Erik's office. "Once that energy is expended we will be brought back here."

"This is a terrible idea, Tristan." Erik steepled his fingers as he leaned back. "The Elders have never been big on conversation and once an edict is given it's never reversed—no matter how wrong it may be."

"It has to be done," Monty said, standing in front of the door. "If you don't mind."

Erik stood with a sigh. "Your funeral." He smoothed out his pants and stepped over to the panel next to the door. "The meet with Anastasia will be set by the time you return—if you return alive."

Monty gave him a short nod.

"Where are they holding Chi?" The door clicked open and I grabbed the handle.

Blood Is Thicker

"You two come back in one piece and I'll share that with you, but you won't like it," Erik said, placing a hand on the door and gesturing. Runes floated into the wood as it opened. "If I were you, I'd start accepting she's gone."

"When I see that with my own eyes, then I'll accept it." I turned the handle and the door flew open as a wind blasted us. "What the hell?"

Erik gave me a tight smile. "Enjoy your trip. Remember, you have thirty minutes." He closed the door behind us as we stepped through. The wind died down almost immediately.

We stood on the summit of a mountain that was covered in grass and shrubbery. A few feet away I could see a pool of clear water. Next to the pool, a pathway led down the mountain. A woman sat in front of the pool with her back to us. The energy signature around her was intense. This was a mage as powerful as Monty, if not more.

"Hello, Tristan," she said without turning. "It's good to see you again."

Monty glanced at me with the 'refrain from pissing her off' look, which I usually disregarded. Except that we were standing on a mountain and I had the distinct feeling that getting her upset would result in us taking the express route down the side of it. I opted to let Monty do all the talking.

<Do you think she has meat?>

"Is that all you think about?" I grabbed Peaches by the scruff and pulled him to the side, away from the woman. She unfolded her legs and stood gracefully as she turned to face us. Her long black hair cascaded behind her as she approached. She wore a long white robe covered in silver runic brocade. I recognized the design from the last gate of the Hellfire Club. Syght had worn the same robes. Unlike Syght, this woman lacked irises.

"Hello, Aria." Monty pulled out the keepsaker from a pocket. "I believe this belongs to you."

Aria extended an arm and Monty placed the box in her open hand. It flared blue for a second and then reverted to normal.

"This was created by a wordweaver, but not an adept." She returned the box to Monty. "This is a crude copy of our boxes. Serviceable, but inferior."

"What happened to your eyes?" I said as Monty sighed next to me. Sometimes the words just escaped my lips. "Who are the wordweavers?"

"*You* must be Simon." Aria turned to me with the hint of a smile. "Since your time is limited, I'll leave that explanation to Tristan. As for my eyes"—she cocked her head to one side as she examined me—"some things are best left unseen."

"Can you tell me who made this?" Monty held up the box.

Aria shook her head slowly. "No, I can only tell you it was an Exiled." She stepped back and placed a hand into the pool as she murmured words under her breath. "No Smith would make that kind of box without the appropriate defenses. That one"—she pointed at the box—"is incomplete."

Monty nodded his head and put the box away. "Thank you, Aria."

"Are you ready?" She moved her hand through the

water as an image began to form in the pool. "The bridge is prepared."

Monty nodded and stepped to the edge of the pool. "This will be keyed to my father under the usual rules?" Monty stepped into the pool as the water parted around his feet.

Aria nodded. "Your ability to cast will be greatly reduced while anchored," Aria said and made another gesture as the image became clearer. "Any large expenditure of energy can sever the bridge, with unpleasant results."

"Understood," Monty said and dived in, disappearing from sight.

<*I don't like getting wet.*>

"You don't have much of a choice," I said and stepped to the edge of the pool with Peaches next to me. "Is this like a teleportation circle?"

"Are you referring to the discomfort after teleporting?" Aria gave a short laugh. "Nausea and the like?"

I nodded. "Exactly. This seems like a long trip and I don't think my body can take it."

"I can assure you, this is nothing like a teleportation circle," she said as the water parted around my feet.

I sighed in relief as the water raced up my legs. I saw Peaches disappear. The water came up to my neck before it stopped. I looked around and saw her focused on me.

"Make sure Tristan doesn't lose control," she said, gesturing to keep the water from moving. "If he severs the bridge, it could kill him."

"Have you met Monty?" I tried to move, but the

water felt thick, holding me in place. "Control is his thing. I don't think he *has* any emotions."

"Be that as it may, he's a mage and he's going to see his Elders." She moved her hand and the water began to slowly rise again. "They have a way of eroding that control. Oh, one more thing, a Smith bridge isn't like a teleportation circle—it's much worse."

The last thing I saw before the water covered me entirely was her smile. Mage humor needed serious work. I felt a pulling on my body as the world went black.

THIRTY

THERE WAS NO way to tell how long I was in the darkness. I opened my eyes and felt the cool stone underneath. I was about to get up when a hand kept me down.

"Wait," Monty said as my stomach and intestines seized. "This is going to be painful."

"Fu—" I started, when my breath left me. My intestines felt like they were being ripped out of my body an inch at a time. I looked down to make sure I didn't have a gaping hole in my abdomen. I closed my eyes and clenched my teeth against the agony. After about a minute, the pain subsided and I was able to breathe regularly. Peaches licked my face once he saw I wasn't groaning in pain.

<*My saliva will help you. A few more licks.*>

"Your drool therapy isn't helping." I pushed him away and sat up. The world still felt wobbly but my insides felt like they were going to remain inside. "Stop licking me."

<Of course it is. You look better now.>

"What I am is a slobbered mess, thanks to you."

<You're welcome.>

He padded away as Monty helped me up. "We need to go see my father and then exit as soon as possible," Monty said as I steadied myself against the wall. "He should be in his chambers."

"Is the trip back going to be like this?" I clutched my stomach and took a few deep breaths. "Because if it is, I'll catch a plane from wherever it is we are."

"There are no airports near here." Monty looked down the corridor we stood in. "We need to move—now."

We walked down the narrow hallway until we came to a large door off to the right. I could see the runes glowing faintly around the doorframe. Monty took a deep breath and pushed the door open. I felt the energy wash over me as we crossed the threshold. The dimly lit room was spacious judging from the echoes of our footsteps.

"You never could take a hint," a voice whispered from the darkness. "Stubborn as your mother."

A trail of runes floated in the air and the room was bathed in a soft golden light. A figure dressed in black robes sat cross-legged on a large cushion in the center of the room. A large hood covered his face.

The room resembled an open-plan loft. A large bed dominated one corner. In the opposite corner, I could see a desk covered with papers and documents. Along one wall, I saw a tall table similar to the one where Monty transformed the fake katana into *kokutan no ken*. In the rear, a doorway seemed to lead off to another room.

"Hello, Father." Monty approached the older man, who stood and pushed back the hood. "You're looking well."

"Tristan…" The old man looked Monty up and down. "What the bloody hell are you doing here? Have you learned nothing? Who's this?" the old man said, looking at me and then pointing at Peaches. "And what's that?"

"Father, this is Simon, my friend." Monty extended a hand in my direction. "Simon, this is my father, Connor Montague, Elder of the Golden Circle," Monty said. "*That* is Peaches, Simon's companion."

Monty had his father's features down to the scowl. The resemblance was unmistakable.

"It's an honor to meet you." I held out my hand. "These are some impressive quarters."

Connor just stared at my hand before turning to Monty. "Are you daft?" Connor said and gestured quickly, his fingers leaving trails of golden light. "He's not even a mage. What were you thinking?"

"Who gave the kill order?" Monty said quietly. "How long have you been held here?"

"Held here?" I said, with a look. "These aren't his quarters?"

"An Elder has quarters five times this size, with several apprentices to assist his work." Monty looked at the space we stood in. "*This* is a cell."

"All the more reason you need to leave—now." Connor gestured again. "Once you came in here you set off the defenses. They will be here shortly. You used a Smith bridge?"

"Yes, but—" Monty started.

"You need to leave." Connor placed his hand on the floor and a teleportation circle materialized around us. "I sent Dex for a reason, Tristan. Listen to him."

"I'll be back." I could hear the edge in Monty's voice. "I'll come back and release you."

"Don't you dare." Connor grabbed Monty by the arm. "Oliver has taken over the Elders. If you return, really return, they'll cut you down the moment you set foot on the mountain. He's the one who gave the order—he's the one sending the Ghosts."

Monty clenched a fist, and I could feel the air around us charge with energy.

"Monty?" I heard the approaching footsteps. "Maybe we should listen to your dad? Those footsteps sound angry."

Black energy formed around Monty's fists. "Let them come," Monty whispered as the energy raced up his arms.

"We can't find Chi if we get shredded here." I unholstered Grim Whisper, and Peaches entered 'pounce and destroy' mode. "We can come back for your dad once we get her safe. I think this calls for a strategic retreat while we still can."

Monty glanced at me. "Your word."

"We *will* come back and free him." I looked at Monty and he nodded. "You have my word."

"You're both fools." Connor grabbed Monty's shoulder. "You stay away, son. They can't hurt me, but they will kill you."

"They'll try," Monty whispered as Connor stepped back, gestured, and activated the teleportation circle.

"I'll come back for you."

The circle flared bright, blinding us as the room disappeared.

THIRTY-ONE

WE ARRIVED IN Erik's office and this time I ejected the contents of my stomach all over his polished wooden floor. When I looked up, I noticed the office was Harlequin-heavy. I counted no less than six of them standing around the room. I dry-heaved a few more times and made my way to one of the wingback chairs. Peaches came over next to me and sat on his haunches.

<Do you need me to lick you better?>

I shook my head and rubbed his. "Not this time, boy."

"That wasn't the anchor." Erik sidestepped my gastric contributions to his office and signaled to a Harlequin, who left the office and returned a few moments later with a large transparent towel. She placed it on the floor, and in seconds, the towel evaporated, removing all traces of my digestive destruction. "How did you return?"

"My father," Monty said, his voice tight, "who is

currently being held *against* his will. An Elder, my *father*, treated like a criminal."

"You can't even think what you're thinking, Tristan." Erik raised a hand and the remaining Harlequins left the office. "The Sanctuary has an army of mages, many of them several orders of power stronger than you. Not to mention the other Elders, who can and *will* erase you before you move a finger."

"What time is the meet with Anastasia?" Monty fished out another one of his wafers and bit off half. Erik raised an eyebrow.

"Dawn tomorrow." Erik walked over to his desk, retrieved the sword case, and handed Monty a piece of paper. "I don't know how you did it, but it passed her test. She'll meet with you there, but you know this is a trap. Once she gets the sword, you're both dead."

Monty nodded, read the paper and handed me the case before finishing the other half of the wafer. "I need to find an Exiled—one of the Smiths. Where are they staying these days?"

"The same place Anastasia wants to meet." Erik sat behind his desk and leaned back. "She's on Ellis Island," he said, looking at me. "That's where she has Michiko, if she's still alive."

"Ellis Island?" Monty rubbed his chin and sat in the other wingback. "That complicates matters."

"Complicates matters?" Erik said, raising his voice. "The island is a death trap. The runic defenses are so thick you'll be lucky if you could create a spark. Do you understand now what you're facing?"

"We need to get her back." I looked at Monty, and he nodded. "Any way around these defenses?"

"*Around*—around the defenses?" Erik stared at me and shook his head. "The island—the *entire* island—is configured with runes. Anastasia didn't pick it by accident. It served as a mage detention site during the war. When it was decommissioned, the Council just shuttered the entire island. No mage is crazy enough to set foot on that island."

"This place is a mage prison?" I glanced at Monty. "You won't be able to cast there."

"Your curse probably won't work there either." Monty looked at the case holding the fake sword. "The illusion I cast on the blade will dissolve faster there as well."

"You're both certifiable." Erik threw his hands in the air. "I don't even know why I bother."

I reached into my jacket and pulled out the pouch holding the battle armor Ken gave me for Michiko. "Do you have anything like this?" I slid the pouch across the desk.

"This is Daystrider Armor." Erik held the fabric between his fingers before sliding the pouch back. "Where did you get this?"

"Ken gave it to me—for Michiko," I said, putting the armor away. "Do you have a mage equivalent or a tank we could use?"

"I'm fresh out of tanks, but I have something close." Erik made a gesture. "Daystrider is the only armor I know that can stop blood arrows." A Harlequin silently stepped into the office a moment later. "Two sets of battle armor. Tristan, do you still remember how to use the blades?"

Monty nodded. "It's been a few years, but it should

come back to me."

"And a pair of Sorrows," Erik said, looking at the Harlequin. The Harlequin bowed and left the room.

"Speaking of blades,"—I tapped Ebonsoul's sheath—"will this work on the island?"

"That weapon predates the island defenses by a few centuries. If any weapon will work there, it should be that one—considering its purpose." Monty stood and pulled on his sleeves. "We need to get back to the office. If we're going to Ellis Island I'm going to need a few things."

I stood up. My stomach felt much calmer. "Thank you, Erik," I said, picking up the sword case and then bowing. "Your help means—"

"I never helped you." Erik stood as the Harlequin entered the office again, holding a narrow bag. "You were never here and we never spoke."

Monty took the narrow bag from the Harlequin and left the office. I followed and stopped at the door for a second. "I'll make sure Michiko knows." I nudged Peaches and continued walking, when Erik spoke.

"Simon, bring her back—alive," Erik whispered as I closed the door behind me.

THIRTY-TWO

I FELT MY phone vibrate as we sped up the West Side Highway. I glanced down and saw Ramirez's number, connected the call and put it on speakerphone.

"Strong, tell me you have answers, something, anything," Ramirez said in his usual 'make my ears bleed' tone. "This Redrum is making the night and days a mess."

"Days?" I swerved around a few cars, and Monty gave me a look. "I thought the blood made them photosensitive?"

"It does," Ramirez said with a sigh. "That's the problem. They feel superhuman until they step into the sun, then it's itching, burning, and boom—Redrum user all over the sidewalk."

"That actually makes sense," Monty said, rubbing his chin. "It's what they want."

"Come again?" Ramirez asked, confused. "What makes sense? Explain it to me. I would love for something to make sense."

It came to me suddenly. "If you wanted to eliminate vampires from the city," I said, braking short and causing a few drivers to give me some New York City blessings, "how would you do it?"

"Fuck me sideways," Ramirez said after a brief pause. "The Blood Hunters are behind this. The brass met with their leader—an Anastasia—a few days ago to discuss the imminent supernatural threat. She said the NYTF was ill-equipped to deal with it."

"They agreed?" I cut off a yellow taxi that proceeded to try to race with me, until I pressed down on the gas. "What did they say?"

"They took it under advisement," Ramirez said. "They don't like anyone pissing in their pool. But some of them are seriously considering working with them."

The NYTF was territorial. If the Blood Hunters came in trying to tell them how to do their jobs, the rank and file would reject them outright. The brass, on the other hand, would 'take it under advisement,' which meant they were looking for a way to turn the situation to their advantage.

"Working with them will end badly." I swerved off the Westside Highway. "We have a meet. Stall the brass until we're done."

"Where's the meet?" Ramirez asked. "Location."

When I didn't answer, he cursed. "Strong, either you tell me where it is or I send out several squads to hunt you down." I heard the punching of keys in the background. "I only need to follow the trail of destruction—your call."

"Ellis Island." I pulled up to the front of the Moscow, took the phone off speaker, and let Peaches out. I walked through the door and noticed Andrei jumped back out of the corner of my eye. I refrained from his regular torture as I headed to the stairs behind Monty with Peaches in tow. "Ramirez?"

"Do you remember when I told you not to go into the Foundry without an army of backup?"

"Vaguely." I climbed the stairs slowly. I knew where this was going. "Chi is on that island, Angel. There is nothing you can say that's—"

"Use the Phoenix Protocol," Ramirez whispered. "I've been doing some digging of my own. Everything about you is scrubbed clean—too clean."

"I can't—shit, Angel," I said with a sigh. "I can't use that without setting off a shitstorm in the NYTF. People would die."

"I know." I could hear the satisfied smirk on his face. "I was just verifying my info. Phoenix Protocols are reserved for higher echelon operatives and Shadow Company. I wonder which you belonged to, Strong?"

"You bastard." I couldn't help the smile on my face. "Stop digging into my past. You won't like what you find."

"I don't like you now," Ramirez answered with a grunt. "Nothing I find is going to make me like you less."

"Don't be so sure." I opened the second-floor door and headed to the office. "What can you tell me about Ellis Island?"

"Officially? Nothing." I heard the keys again. "Unofficially, I'd tell you to stay away even though I know you won't. It's a Dark Council black site. It has been shut down for decades. No one goes there. The place is so jammed up with old energy it fries anyone who tries to use magic while standing on it."

"Runic defenses." I looked around but didn't see Monty or Dex. Peaches headed for his food bowl and began to vacuum-inhale his food. "Any way around those? I would prefer to remain unfried."

"Bullets and blades," Ramirez said. "Make sure Tristan keeps his magic in check. The defenses are nasty. Are you sure she's on that island?'

"Ninety percent." I heard a noise coming from the guest bedroom. I saw the narrow case the Harlequin gave Monty resting next to the door. "I'll be careful. If I see it's too hot, we'll bail out."

We both knew it was a lie and he gave me a short laugh.

"Bullshit," Ramirez said and then lowered his voice. "If anyone can get on and off that place in one piece it's you two. NYTF isn't even supposed to sneeze in that direction but I can swing some unofficial *consultants*—if you need them."

"Too dangerous." I stopped in front of the guestroom door. "The meet is tomorrow at dawn. I'll call you after."

"If you don't, I'm launching an S and R to recover your body."

"Your confidence inspires me." The door rattled in the frame. "Listen, I've got to go."

"Make sure you call me when you get safe," Ramirez said before we disconnected.

I pulled open the door and my brain seized for a few seconds as I looked out over a large courtyard enclosed by wide stone columns. Etched into the ground in front of each column, I saw a circle made of runes. I looked back into our office and shook my head.

"What the fu—?" A blast of air shoved me back into the office, causing a fireball to miss me. The heat embraced me as the fireball evaporated. I looked across the courtyard to see Dex forming another orb of flame.

"A simple no would've sufficed," Monty said as he stepped in front of me. "Simon, you may want to step back. He's being difficult."

I unsheathed Ebonsoul and saw Dex smile.

"That's the spirit!" Dex yelled from across the courtyard. "He may be daft, but at least the boy has stones. You, on the other hand,"—he pointed at Monty—"I'm not so sure."

Dex released the fireball and it raced at Monty. As it approached, it split into three fireballs. They swerved and homed in on Monty, who stepped out of the courtyard and closed the door behind him. The fireballs thudded into the door in rapid succession.

I sheathed Ebonsoul as Dex walked into the office a few seconds later. "Tristan, you're throwing your life away for a vampire?" Dex barked. He turned and looked at me. "No offense, lad. I know you're sweet on her—but a vampire? Heed me, this will not end well." He was topless and wearing a black-and-red kilt. The rune-scars across his torso gave off a faint green light. Herk flew in low and perched on the branch he held with a squawk as the door closed with a bang behind him.

"Aren't you involved with the Morrigan?" I pointed at the raven that glared at me with its green eyes. "That seems like a bad idea any way you try and sell it."

Dex cursed under his breath and stalked off only to come back a few seconds later. "That's different." He pointed at me with his branch. "What she and I have is—"

"Complicated," I finished. "Doesn't make it any less real. Vampire, or insane goddess of the dead."

"'The blood of the covenant is thicker than the water of the womb,'" Monty said, his voice steel. "You taught me that. Those were your words."

"I know they're my words—I said them!" Dex threw up his hands and cursed again. "*Eich bod yn y ddau wallgof*—both of you are insane."

"We leave in the morning," Monty said with a smile and removed the battle armor from the narrow case by the door. He grabbed the remaining set and handed it to me. Next to the armor, I saw the gleam of two short swords—the Sorrows.

"There's no casting for you on that island," Dex said seriously. "I hope you have another method of using your abilities."

Monty pointed at the case. "I have those.

Dex looked into the narrow case, saw the swords, and grunted. "Oi, you still know how to use them?" he said, removing one of the blades. He swung it in the air and the sound it made took me by surprise. Each practice cut he executed sounded like the weeping of a young girl.

"I'm sure it'll come back to me." Monty removed the second blade and held it out, checking the balance. "These will allow me to cast without fatal backlash."

Black runes covered the silver blade on both sides.

The hilt was the figure of a young woman with her arms outstretched to the sides. When Monty extended the sword, the figure's arms wrapped loosely around his wrist. Dex turned the sword he held and handed it to Monty, hilt-first.

"Those are fine weapons." Dex pointed at me. "What are you bringing?"

"I'm ready." I moved my jacket to the side to show him Grim Whisper. "Entropy rounds."

"Entropy rounds—impressive." Dex nodded his head in approval. "What happens when you run out of bullets? You're going to stop them with your charm bracelet?"

"If I have to, yes." I adjusted the mala bracelet on my wrist. "I also have this." I unsheathed Ebonsoul.

Dex whistled under his breath and held out his hand. "May I?" I handed him the blade and he turned it over. He narrowed his eyes at me and looked at Monty, who nodded.

"He's bonded to it," Monty said and placed the swords across his back in a cross sheath. "Don't ask me how."

"Bonded to a dark blade and still sane—well, relatively sane," Dex said with a grin. "We may walk off the island after all."

"What are you bringing?" I asked, sheathing Ebonsoul as Dex handed it back. "Besides bad jokes."

Monty glared at me. "I apologize, Uncle Dex," Monty said quickly. "His brain occasionally malfunctions and his mouth takes over—"

Dex held up a hand and Monty fell silent. "It's a fair question," Dex said, never taking his eyes off me.

"Especially if one's life hangs in the balance."

I immediately regretted my question as I felt the energy around me build. Dex just smiled at me, but it wasn't a friendly 'I'd like to get to know you' smile. This was closer to a 'the next few seconds are the last ones of your life' smile. Real fear gripped me as Dex extended his arms.

"Uncle Dex?" Monty said warily and stepped closer to me. "He doesn't know the customs."

Dex ignored Monty and kept staring at me. "If we're going to share blood on a battlefield, you should know who stands by your side," Dex said in a low voice. "To me, Herk!"

The raven flapped over, sat on his shoulder, and dug in with its talons. Blood flowed freely as the raven spread its wings and shifted, growing even larger. A green flash blinded me and the raven was gone. Dex's body was covered entirely in black feathers with a metallic sheen. Only his glowing green eyes were visible. He grabbed his branch with both hands and held it in front of him. I saw Monty gesture as a shield formed around us.

"You had to ask?" Monty said as he kept gesturing and moving us back. Even with shield and distance, I felt the power coming off Dex. "He's one of the strongest mages in the Golden Circle."

"This is what I bring," Dex said, his voice low. He raised the staff several feet off the floor. "I bring power."

He slammed the staff down in the best Gandalf 'you shall not pass' move I'd ever seen. The shockwave tossed Monty and me like ragdolls across the room. I swear I felt the building shake. By the time my vision cleared, the raven armor was gone and Dex stood facing us with a huge grin.

"That—was *epic*." I stood up and straightened out my jacket. "Tolkien would be proud."

"Oh no," Monty muttered under his breath behind me. "Don't get him started."

"First off"—Dex held up a finger—"I had to convince him to shorten that tongue twister of a name —John Ronald Reuel—to J.R.R.," Dex said, opening the door to his room. "If you survive tomorrow, I'll tell you how I helped him create his wizard."

"You helped him create Gandalf?"

"Boy, I'm the reason Tolkien even *wrote* a Gandalf." Dex looked at me and grew serious. "Do you still want to know what I'll be bringing?"

I shook my head. "No, thank you," I said. "I have an idea now."

Dex gave me a short nod and a sly grin. "Next time you come into my quarters I'd advise you to knock first." He stepped into his room and I swear I could see a green field with a castle in the distance before he closed the door behind him.

"We'd better get some sleep." Monty stepped next to me. "Everything hinges on tomorrow."

THIRTY-THREE

IMPENDING DEATH BRINGS you clarity of thought and purpose. I rarely gave much thought to my life ending. Being immortal has a way of shoving that to the back of your mind. In a few hours, I was going to step on an island so covered in magic that I might be rendered mortal. There was a good chance I wasn't coming back from this. Love and insanity are thinly separated emotions. Over time, it's hard to tell them apart.

I put on the battle armor. It was lighter than Kevlar and reminded me of articulated dragonskin combined with chainmail. It covered me from the neck down. A hood provided a snug fit to protect from headshots. I could see the faintly glowing runes shimmer across its dark surface and hoped they could stop blood arrows.

I strapped on Grim Whisper's shoulder holster, tightened the thigh sheath holding Ebonsoul, and attached the flask of Valhalla Java to my other leg. I headed to the conference room, where I heard voices.

<Are we going out?>

Peaches bumped into my leg, nearly dislocating my knee as I rounded the corner. I avoided smashing my face into the wall by turning and letting my shoulder take the brunt of the impact. His playful taps were getting dangerous. For a second I considered leaving him in the office. Then I remembered what he did to Roxanne. I doubted he would remain behind.

"We need to go get Chi, boy." I rubbed his head as he rumbled at me. "I need you to stay close to me. This is going to be dangerous."

<Can the birdman make more meat?>

"I'll ask him." We entered the conference room.

Monty and Dex were discussing Ziller's theorems of teleportation circles and the displacement of mass. Monty had tried to explain this to me once when I asked about the wonderful aftereffects of teleportation. I wasn't going to subject myself to the torture a second time. I pulled out Grim Whisper and checked it again.

On the table in front of them was a large map of Ellis Island. The island was U-shaped and turned on its side. Buildings occupied both ends of the U. The north side held the Immigration Museum. Several other buildings were connected to this main structure. The south side held the Ellis Island Hospital Morgue—a sprawling complex of small buildings. In the center of the U sat a large, squat building with a dock leading right into the water. It connected both ends of the island. Behind this building, the map showed a bridge leading away from the island and into New Jersey.

"If we land on the south side," Monty said, pointing at the map, "we can secure the hospital area and use it as a base of operations."

"Base of operations?" Dex scoffed. "You have an army I'm not seeing? There's three of us."

Peaches rumbled.

"Four of us."

The raven squawked and flapped its wings.

"Five of us," Dex said and looked around. "Five of us. We use stealth and the element of surprise and storm the main building."

"We need to draw them here." I pointed to the bridge. "Dex, can Herk pull a Hugin and Munin?"

"A what?" Dex looked at me and then smiled as he nodded. "Aye, that he can do."

"We send him first and recon the island." I looked down at the map. "If you port Dex and the animals in this corner,"—I pointed to the northeast corner covered in trees—"they can find where Michiko is being held and target that area. How far out does the dampening effect extend? Does it cover the bridge?"

"Only the island is affected," Monty said, rubbing his chin. "I should be able to cast on the bridge. I would say mid-span just to be safe. The problem would be getting the Blood Hunters off the island."

"I'm going to call in a favor." I rubbed my mark and hoped my idea would work. If it didn't, we were all dead. "Where are we meeting her?"

"Anastasia wants to meet here." Monty pointed to the center building that joined the island. "We'll be vulnerable from every angle. What favor? From whom?"

"Anastasia isn't expecting Dex." I shifted to one side to get a better look at the map. "Once he finds Chi, he can unleash *the power*,"—I gave Dex a sidelong glance—"grab her and get to the bridge."

"And then what?" Monty looked at the map. "There's nothing around the bridge—no cover, no egress. The Blood Hunters will attack en mass."

"I'm counting on it," I answered. "Do you think you can teleport something as large as the Goat?"

"I can't." Monty shook his head and pointed at Dex. "But he can. And for the record, this plan is insane."

"I like the way you think, boy." Dex grinned at me. "I'll find your vampire. Why are we taking a goat? Are sacrifices required?"

"I'll explain on the way," I said and nearly fell over from another nudge from Peaches. "Dex, do you think you can make another one of your sausages—to go?"

THIRTY-FOUR

"HOW CLOSE DO we need to be?" I parked the car behind the US Coast Guard Recruiting Center next to the South Ferry and looked across the water to Ellis Island. "That's a lot of water to cross."

"Things like distance, space, and time are flexible constructs," Dex said, getting out of the car. "Ziller postulates that—wait, have you studied Ziller?"

"Only when I want my brain melted." I walked over to the edge of the parking lot. The sky was growing lighter as dawn approached. "You're going to have to magicscience the hell out of this. Can you do it?"

"A split teleportation sending you and Tristan to one location," —he gestured and a large rune-filled circle appeared around the Goat—"your vehicle to another, and myself and these creatures to a third location?"

Two more circles appeared equidistant from the car. "Have you done this before?" I said, looking at the circles warily. "I mean, you have done this before, right?"

"The theory is sound." Dex nodded and stepped into one of the circles with Peaches padding next to him and sitting on his haunches. Dex motioned for Monty and me to enter the other. "Let's see if this works," Dex said and scrunched up his face as he scratched his head.

"He does know what he's doing?" I took the sword case from Monty, and then I looked over the expanse of water and braced myself for gastrointestinal grief. "This is going to suck."

"This is my first time trying a three-way teleport," Dex stage-whispered, looking down at Peaches. "I hope I remember the sequences." The pouch holding Chi's Daystrider Armor was strapped to Peaches' back. Dex extended his arms as Herk covered him with a green flash.

I stared at Monty. "Tell me this is more mage humor," I said as my stomach clenched in anticipation.

"He's actually a master of multiple teleportation," Monty said, adjusting the swords on his back. "He used to practice with us when we were children."

"Ach!" Dex said and scowled at Monty. "Your sense of humor is as keen as ever, Tristan. About as fun as sitting on a sharp stick."

Monty ignored him. "You can imagine the hours of childhood pleasure as he teleported us all over the Sanctuary," Monty continued. "Many times we would wander into his teleportation circles unknowingly and find ourselves on different parts of the mountain or in the middle of the lake."

Dex grinned at me and shrugged. "I may have understated my abilities a bit." He began to gesture.

"It's not proper to think too highly of one's ability, you know. Pride goeth before the slippery slope of destruction—or something like that."

I smiled in spite of myself. "That's not even close." I felt the tugging of the circle as the runes flared around my feet. "Remember—find Chi and get to the car. Try not to die."

Peaches chuffed at me.

"Keep them safe, boy," I said, checking my weapons one last time. "Find Chi."

<*I will find the angry lady.*>

"May we get what we want, may we get what we need," Dex said with a grin as his gestured again. "But may we never get what we deserve." He placed his hands together and the world went white.

When the world came back into focus, Monty and I were standing on the side of the bridge closest to Ellis Island. I stood still, waiting for the eventual gut punch, but it never came.

"I told you he was a master of teleportation." Monty started walking toward Ellis Island. "Your intestines are safe for now."

"So all my digestive distress is because you suck at teleportation?" I stood still and held my stomach gingerly in case there was a delayed reaction.

"That plus your delicate and weak constitution." Monty walked ahead.

I looked behind us and could just make out the silhouette of the Goat sitting in the middle of the bridge. It flared orange for a second and I thought the lock had activated. It was actually the first rays of the sun climbing over the horizon. I rushed to catch up to

Monty.

On the tops of the buildings, I could see the figures holding both long and crossbows. Erik wasn't kidding when he said they were an army. I counted no less than twenty and we weren't even on the island proper yet. Every building I scanned had two or more Blood Hunters on the roof. I noticed two things right away. All of them were female, and they all had arrows trained on us.

"You think they all carry blood arrows?" I asked as we crossed the bridge. "Maybe some of them have the regular non-blow-you-up arrows?"

Monty gave me the 'stop being dense' look and pointed forward with his chin. "Focus," he whispered under his breath. "We have company."

I looked ahead and saw three figures approach the bridge. I didn't recognize two of them. The center one made my hand slide closer to Ebonsoul.

"Esti." I kept my hand away from my weapons through sheer force of will. She was dressed in her black bodysuit. All of the Blood Hunters wore some variation of the same. The sections of ballistic armor that covered parts of her body were black, but some of the other Blood Hunters wore gray or brown. I guessed she didn't have time to do her makeup. Her face, neck, and arms were bare of any paint this time. She sniffed the air and stepped closer.

"You came to witness your last sunrise beside your *beloved vampire*?" She spat the last words. "The blades."

"When I see her, you get the blades, not before," I said, staring her down. "Where is Anastasia?"

"Follow me," Esti said and turned. "I will take you

to both, and an old friend of yours."

The Blood Hunter on the right approached and made to remove Monty's swords.

"Touch my weapons and that will be the last thing you ever touch," Monty whispered as he kept walking. The Blood Hunter backed off with a snarl.

Esti waved her hand. "Allow them their weapons," she said with a laugh. "They can do nothing here today —except die."

I glanced upward and saw a large bird flying over the island. Some of the Blood Hunters glanced at it, but none took their arrows off us. We arrived at the main building.

"How's the magic?" I whispered under my breath. "Anything?"

Monty shook his head as we kept walking. The building consisted of a central atrium where immigrants were processed. The façade of the building was made up of three immense windows. Blood Hunters stood all around the atrium with arrows drawn. I looked around, but I didn't see Chi.

Against the far wall, opposite the windows, sat a woman. If Esti was a loose cannon, this woman was a sniper bullet. She wore the black Blood Hunter bodysuit, but her ballistic armor was golden. Taut muscles flexed as she brought her hands together, interlacing her fingers. Her dark eyes focused on us as we approached. I could see her assessing what kind of threat we were, but her face was a stone mask, giving away nothing.

An array of daggers rested on the side of each thigh as she crossed her long legs. Across her back, I could see the hilt of a large sword. She sat in a large oak chair and made it look like a throne. On either side of the chair stood six Blood Hunters, swords drawn and held across their chests. Their ballistic armor was red and I assumed this was an elite guard. As dangerous as they appeared, they paled in comparison to the relaxed lethality this woman projected.

Esti stepped close to the chair and bowed. "*Señora, el mago y su compañero,*" the mage and his partner.

"*Gracias, Esti. Buscame el traidor,*" the woman replied with a wave of her hand. "I am Anastasia Anyxia Santiago, leader of the *Cazadoras Sangrientas*—you call us the Blood Hunters, but we hunt the true danger. I believe you have something that belongs to me."

I gave the case to the Blood Hunter who approached. She opened it and removed the fake *kokutan no ken*. She handed it to Anastasia hilt-first as I heard a struggle behind us. The black blade gleamed in the low light of the atrium and I held my breath as she held it up to her face.

"Get your hands off me!" I heard the familiar male voice yell. "We had a deal. I held up my end of the bargain."

It was Nick. Esti dragged him in front of Anastasia and pushed him down on his knees. On this island there would be no way for him to plane-weave or use any of his magic. He was trapped.

"Where is the second?" Anastasia said, looking at me as she stood and walked over to where Nick knelt. Every step whispered of death. Watching her move was mesmerizing. It was like watching a cobra before it struck, or a lioness stalk prey. Now I knew why Esti was second to her. I had no doubt Anastasia could erase Esti with little effort. I moved my hand slowly and pointed to Ebonsoul.

"Where is Chi?" I said, my voice full of menace. "You give her to me and I hand this over."

"You believe you're in a position to bargain?" she said with a smile that chilled my blood. "How charming. You have come here to rescue your damsel in distress. Is that it?"

I could feel the rage rising.

"We have come here to negotiate her release," Monty said calmly. "It would be preferable to do this without bloodshed."

"Your threats are empty and your weapons useless on this island, mage." Anastasia pointed to the large windows with the fake sword. "Your vampire is ready to greet the morning sun. Say your goodbyes—while you still can."

I followed the sword up to where she pointed and there, strapped to the center window, was Chi. That's when I realized that we were facing east. The rising sun. Realization struck me then.

"You bitch," I said, but remained motionless, "you were never going to let her go."

I saw the sky getting lighter. Soon the sun would creep over the horizon and turn Chi to dust. Inside, the rage started to break free. I wasn't going to let that happen.

"Let her go? Are you insane?" Anastasia laughed. "We are Blood Hunters! We have a singular purpose. We exist to eliminate vampires and *all* who help them."

"We had a deal, I held up my end," Nick said again

with a sob. "Let me go. I gave you the vials and the boxes. Just like you asked. The streets are full of Redrum."

"Yes, Wraith, you held up your end," Anastasia said softly. "Thanks to you, we will have plenty of creatures to hunt. The NYTF will beg us to cleanse this city of their kind. But I have a little problem—I can't trust you, Nicholas. You betrayed your own kind."

She raised his head with the tip of the blade. "You can trust me—I mean I did what you asked, didn't I?" Nick said, obviously not realizing his life was ending. "If you let me go I can still help you. I can still get more vials. I have connections—connections you can use."

Anastasia walked a few steps away and then stopped. "I think I *will* let you go, Nicholas." Nick smiled at her words, a glimmer of hope in his eyes. She spun around faster than my eye could track and turned to face me. Behind her, Nick's head slid off his body with a wet thud. His face still held the smile of hope at her words. "You can never trust a traitor. Sooner or later they turn on you."

"That's what I call severance pay." I moved my hand to cover my mark. Everything depended on her showing up. "I promise to kill you quickly—if you give me Chi."

"I think you overestimate your position," Anastasia said and headed back to her chair. She sat down, crossed her legs, and rested the fake sword across the arms of the chair. "We will watch your vampire greet the sun, you will both join Nicholas, and then we will purge this city of the vampire scum."

Blood Is Thicker

Two Blood Hunters approached and directed us to face the window and the approaching dawn, before stepping back several feet. I looked up and saw Chi struggle against the bonds, but I couldn't see her face.

Erik's words came back to me: *You don't reason with them, you don't appeal to their sense of right and wrong. They are relentlessly driven to achieve one goal. Nothing can stop them except their own annihilation.*

I pressed the mark on my hand and nothing happened.

"Oh, shit," I muttered under my breath. "We are truly fucked."

"Remember what I told you—there's one weapon here that will work despite the defenses of the island," Monty said and glanced down at my thigh sheath. "You need to use that first."

"On myself?" I hissed. "Are you serious?"

"Or we can watch your vampire die," Monty whispered back. "Whatever you're going to do, make it quick. We're running out of time."

If I moved to draw Ebonsoul, I would resemble a porcupine in a matter of seconds. I needed a way to draw the blade and use it without becoming a blood-arrow pincushion—and Monty was right. I was running out of time. Then it hit me.

"Señora," I said with a deep bow and faced Anastasia, "may I approach?"

"No, say what you need to say from there," she said with a glare. Easily four Eastwoods on the glare-o-meter, but I deducted two because, well, she was a bitch.

I needed to be convincing. "I don't agree with

anything you've said, but I do know one thing—this doesn't belong to me," I said and slowly drew Ebonsoul. "I offer it to you in exchange for the release of my friend. He never approved of my relationship with Chi."

Anastasia nodded and a Blood Hunter approached. I needed to make this look like an accident or the arrows would fly. I held Ebonsoul by the blade with my marked hand. When the Blood Hunter pulled the blade from my fingers, I held on just a bit tighter than necessary, slicing my palm.

"Señora, forgive me," the Blood Hunter said. "I did not mean—"

"You fool," Anastasia said and narrowed her eyes. Her expression went from mild displeasure to rage. "Kill them!"

I pressed the mark and white light shot out from the top of my left hand. Everything around me was slightly out of focus and frozen. I looked around and admired the massive amounts of arrows headed our way. The elite guard had detached and approached, swords ready. Esti had knives in both her hands and was closing. Even Anastasia had gotten out of her chair, black blade gleaming, ready to remove more body parts.

"Splinter," the familiar voice said from behind me, and I braced myself. I still had to get her to agree. "I see you are trying new and novel ways to test your immortality. Are those blood arrows?"

The smell of lotus blossoms wafted by my nose, the scent laden with citrus and mixed with an enticing hint of cinnamon. This was followed by the sweet smell of wet earth after a hard rain.

Blood Is Thicker

"Hello, Karma." I turned slowly in case she was feeling handy and decided to introduce me to one of her bone-cracking slaps of greeting. She was dressed in vintage brown motorcycle leathers complete with leather cap, which read BITCH across the visor.

"You summoned me," she said, her voice hard. "Even after I expressly advised you against it. Why would you risk your life this way? You do recall you're not immortal in this state?"

I pointed to the window holding Chi. "Dawn is a few minutes away."

Karma stepped close and placed a hand on my cheek. I flinched reflexively, and she smiled. "You would risk your life for her?" She looked around and shook her head. "Obviously that's a rhetorical question. Are you aware she's a vampire?"

I almost answered in my typical fashion and then I remembered I was dealing with the embodiment of causality, so I just nodded. This probably saved my life.

"You still don't see it?" Karma said. "This isn't just an attack on the Dark Council or vampires. It goes deeper."

"Deeper?"

"Find the commonality, Splinter. Out of all the vampires on the Council, why target her?"

"She heads the Council," I said, confused. "That makes her a target."

"No." She tapped me lightly and stars raced across my vision. "Stop being dense. Do you see any Council members here? No. They were willing to let her die."

"I'm not seeing it," I said, acutely aware of the cloud of arrows pointed in my direction. "It may have something to do with the swarm of blood arrows heading my way."

"That *is* a lot of arrows." Karma nodded and looked around. "Looks like you're honing your gift for pissing off the wrong people."

"I can't see it," I said, frustrated. "I'm sorry."

"Until you make the connection, you and everyone around you will be vulnerable," Karma said and adjusted her cap. "Now, what do you want?"

"Can you get Chi down from there?" I looked up to the window. "There's no way I can reach her in time."

"Once time flows again, that will be handled by the old man," she said with a sly smile. "What do you *really* want?"

I tried opening with the emotional request, expecting her to be moved: it didn't work.

"I need the island defenses down for thirty minutes." I stared into her bottomless eyes. "I need Monty and Dex to be able to access their magic while on the island."

"And by default have your curse active?"

I nodded. "Can you do it?"

This time she did slap me across the floor. "Don't ever question my abilities or, even worse, try to goad me into taking an action—understood?" she said as she stepped over to where I lay and picked me up by my neck.

I spit blood on the floor. "Understood," I croaked around her vice-like grip. She loosened her hand slightly when I started to see spots and my vision began tunneling in.

"I can suspend the defenses for ten minutes, but

longer than that and the karmic repercussions will demand I balance the outcomes in every branch of causality stemming from the suspension—which means a colossal pain in my ass." Karma dropped me on the floor. "Greater even than dealing with you. Take it or leave it. Though I suggest you take it and move the mage before the flow is restored."

"Thank you," I said as I relocated Monty away from the arrows. I grabbed Ebonsoul from the Blood Hunter who had pulled it from my hand.

"I hate zealots, so don't thank me," Karma said with a smile and a tip of her visor as she gestured to the Blood Hunters around the atrium. "You still have to deal with all of that."

She turned with a wave and disappeared. Time snapped back and chaos took over.

There was a good reason archers never stand in a circle to bring down an enemy. If for some reason the enemy manages to avoid the arrows, the archers are now essentially shooting each other. It becomes the worst case of unfriendly fire when you realize an explosive arrow is buried in your leg and your fellow archer put it there.

Several of the Blood Hunters found themselves in this situation, but I couldn't devote any mental energy to them. The shattering of glass forced me to look up. A giant raven grabbed Chi and fell to the ground, tumbling across the atrium.

"You did this? How?" Monty said next to me as he took in the utter confusion. "Have I mentioned how fearsome you can be?"

"I called in a favor," I said, dodging a sword thrust

from a passing Blood Hunter. "Defenses go back up in ten minutes. Until then, you have—"

I saw him hurl several fireballs as he superheated the air around him. "Go get your vampire," he said and unleashed several orbs of air, slamming Blood Hunters into the walls.

I ran to where Michiko and the raven landed, only it wasn't Herk, it was Dex. I saw she was wearing the Daystrider Armor, but I didn't see Peaches. When she didn't move, I feared the worst.

"She's still alive, but it doesn't look good, lad," Dex said, his voice grim. "They starved and beat her to an inch of her sanity. If she regains consciousness, she'll be more of a threat than the Blood Hunters."

"I need you to get her to the car." I looked around the fray. Monty was dealing with most of the Blood Hunters. I didn't see Anastasia or Esti. I handed Dex my flask. "This is Valhalla Brew. Give her a few drops at a time until she stabilizes, but don't let her regain consciousness. Can you keep her under?"

Dex nodded. "I can be more help here," Dex said, looking around the atrium. "I can *bring the power*."

I grabbed him by the arm to get his attention. "Listen to me. The defenses will only be down for a few more minutes," I said with urgency. "We need to be off this island by then. Help me do that."

Dex nodded and scooped up Chi. I touched her cheek one last time before he ran out of the building, with Herk flapping behind him.

"Where are you, boy?" I said out loud, looking around the atrium for a four-legged agent of destruction. I saw him in the corner as he pounced on a Blood Hunter and launched her into a column, cracking it. She crumpled to the floor and he ran in my direction, barreling down another Blood Hunter in the process.

<*I'm here. I've been biting a lot of the bad ladies. Birdman said it was okay.*>

"That's good, boy." I scanned the atrium and found the side exit Anastasia and Esti must have used. "We need to find a few more. Ready?"

Peaches barked in response and several panes of glass shattered as I winced. Monty looked in our direction and nodded. He would catch up when he was finished. I ran for the side exit with Peaches next to me.

THIRTY-FIVE

THE SIDE EXIT led to another, smaller, atrium. In the center stood Anastasia. She must have sent Esti on ahead. I would catch her later.

"Kali's chosen," Anastasia sneered and drew her other sword, tossing the fake *kokutan no ken* to one side. I paused in my approach. "Oh yes, I know all about you, immortal."

Seriously, the leaks about my condition were getting out of control. "Then you know you should quit now while you're behind." Peaches rumbled next to me. "Be careful with her, boy. She's dangerous."

"I don't know how you managed to disable the defenses, but even now I can feel them returning," Anastasia said as a black flame enveloped her sword. "I wonder, are you still immortal in the absence of magic?"

Her sword looked dangerous without the flames. The flames just convinced me that staying away was the best strategy. I pulled Grim Whisper and emptied the magazine. She held the sword in front of her, deflecting all of the rounds.

"A null sword—totally not fair," I said and holstered my gun, drawing Ebonsoul. "Are you sure you don't want to surrender?"

She slid forward and lunged, faster than I expected. Faster than any human had the right to be. A smile crossed her lips as she circled around me. It was the smile of 'I know something you don't and it's going to get you killed.' I hated that smile. Sunlight streamed in through the large windows and I realized how bad the situation really was. When Anastasia crossed into the sunlight, her skin turned that black inky color I thought was camouflage paint. It wasn't paint. The designs etched into her skin were runes.

She sliced horizontally and I managed to get Ebonsoul up in time to parry. The force of her blow sent me across the floor.

"I hunt and kill creatures ten times faster than you," she said and closed the distance. "You're outclassed, outgunned, and outmatched. Why not surrender and let me end your pitiful existence?"

"It must really suck to be a vampire hunter and have one of the most powerful vampires escape right in front of your face," I said as she feinted. "Must make you feel like a rank amateur. A noob, even."

"Your vampire didn't escape." She slashed down as I barely sidestepped. I unleashed a kick to her midsection, which she blocked with a forearm. Peaches launched himself at her and she swatted him away. He rolled away from the blow and stalked back, growling. "I tasked Esti with ending her. Your vampire should be dead by now."

"Not quite," said a voice from the doorway.

Esti's body flew into the center of the atrium and slid across the floor. I could tell right away that both of her arms were broken. Several stiletto blades were buried in her legs and only her ragged breathing gave any indication she was still alive.

Michiko stepped into the atrium, followed by Dex. I gave him the stink-eye. "I thought I told you to keep her under?"

He shrugged at me and shook his head. Michiko picked up the fake *kokutan no ken*, hefted it in her hand, and nodded. "This will be adequate," Chi said, never taking her eyes off Anastasia. "Simon, I will need assistance with this Blood Hunter. Do you feel up to the task?"

"Like I have a choice?" I muttered.

"You don't," Chi answered. "If I fall, she will kill you, your mage, your creature, and the old man along with his deranged bird. Together you and I can stop her."

"Hey," Dex said in an offended voice, "I'm not *that* old."

"Go find Monty," I said, still giving him attitude. "The defenses are coming back up. You can 'bring the power' all you want now."

He left the way he came, and Anastasia smiled at us. "A vampire and her thrall?" Anastasia said, circling around and keeping us in front of her. "This is insulting. I have eliminated entire clans of vampire filth."

Michiko moved then. She slid forward and evaded

several thrusts. Anastasia blocked her attack and launched several daggers at me. I parried them away and they exploded when they contacted the wall. Michiko leaped away from a flurry of attacks. I slid in and face-blocked a backfist that slid me across the floor. I was holding back and it was going to get me killed.

I had to let go and let Ebonsoul take over. I ran at Anastasia and ducked under a swipe from her null sword. I managed to slice across her leg, but her armor protected her from the cut. She spun into a back kick and buried her foot in my ribs, cracking a few, and launched me into a wall.

Michiko pressed the attack, but I could tell through the haze of pain that she was in trouble. Anastasia was exceptional and Michiko was recovering and fighting during the day. This could only end one way and Anastasia knew it.

She launched an attack and forced Michiko into a defensive position. It was only a matter of time before Chi made a mistake. Anastasia closed the distance, driving a fist into Michiko's midsection. Michiko doubled over and immediately reversed direction as Anastasia kneed her in the face, sending Michiko into a wall.

"Hey," I said through clenched teeth, "come pick on someone taller."

I staggered to my feet and felt my body flush with heat as my ribs reset into place, the pain astounding me into breathlessness. As the agony washed over me, something snapped, and I released the rage. Ebonsoul came alive in my hands. I saw the runes flare to life as

Anastasia closed in on me.

"Impossible," Anastasia said as she lunged at me. "How did you bond to it? You're not worthy. You're vampire-loving scum. You deserve to die just like the rest of them!"

I parried her lunge, rotated around her, and slashed across. Ebonsoul cut through her armor, bone, and muscle in one stroke. She fell forward, clutching her throat with a look of surprise as she bled out.

I collapsed just as Monty and Dex entered the atrium. In the distance, I heard the whirring of helicopters and I knew the NYTF would be all over the scene in minutes. They'd have questions. Questions I couldn't answer right now, especially with a building full of dead and broken Blood Hunters.

"We need to go—now." I stumbled to the exit. Monty held me up as we made it to the car. "No way I'm driving," I said, lying in the back next to Michiko and Peaches, who refused to give up more than half the back seat, the selfish mutt.

Monty started the Goat and floored the gas. Two seconds later, we screeched to a stop. I squinted through the windshield and saw a man dressed in a black suit and gold tie standing in the center of the bridge. He held an immense orb of red energy, easily the size of the Goat, over his head.

"Oliver sends his regards, Tristan," the man said with a self-satisfied smile.

"That doesn't look friendly," I said and grabbed my mala bracelet. "Is that a Ghost?"

"Oh, bugger," Dex said and began gesturing. "This is going to hurt."

Monty floored the gas as the man released the orb. We raced across the bridge as the angry red orb of energy crashed into the Goat. For a second, time stood still and held its breath. I looked around the inside of the car. Monty held the steering wheel in a white-knuckle death grip. Dex gestured furiously, as green trails of energy followed his fingers.

Next to me, Michiko gripped the handle of the door, an expression of controlled fury on her face. Peaches had shifted into 'pounce and obliterate' mode and moved closer to me, sensing my agitation. I pressed the main bead on my mala bracelet as the Goat launched backward. The shield materialized and I faced the rear, expecting the worst when we landed. Time exhaled and it was violent.

The inside of the car was a runic spectrum of color as we sailed back onto Ellis Island. The Goat landed, bounced, and rolled several times before coming to a sudden stop against the main building.

Pain squeezed my body as we opened the doors and tumbled out. I looked in wonder as the Goat sat there unscratched and intact.

"How the hell—?" I stumbled to my feet, still dazed from the rough landing.

"Move, boy!" yelled Dex as he grabbed me and shoved me out of the way. Another orb, this one black, crashed into the Goat, which bubbled and steamed as it started to dissolve.

"What the hell was that?" I asked, shocked that anything could damage my beloved car. "It's destroying the Goat."

"Ach!" Dex spat. "They sent a dark one. This is

going to be nasty. We need to get off this island."

"How did he...?" I looked at the rapidly disintegrating car. "He killed the Goat!

"He overwhelmed the defenses and then exploited the weakness," Monty said and withdrew the swords from his back—the Sorrows. Dex gripped his staff. In the distance, the man on the bridge began walking toward us at a leisurely pace. Dressed in a dark suit and gold tie, he reminded me of Ian, the recently deceased Arbiter.

"This is a bad idea." I looked at Chi, who was wobbly on her feet and having trouble dealing with the sun. The Daystrider Armor protected her, but I could tell she was getting weaker. "She needs medical attention—we all do."

"The boy's right," Dex said and looked at Monty, who nodded. "We need to slow the bugger down."

"I'll deal with the bridge, you handle our exit," Monty said and raced to the edge of the bridge. The man, seeing Monty run, picked up his pace and started advancing on us. Dex stepped to the side and slammed his staff into the stone, burying it halfway.

"This is going to turn your insides out, but it can't be helped," he said with a gesture. A large green teleportation circle formed around the staff as he extended an arm. "Herk!"

The raven swooped in and perched on his arm, digging its talons into his forearm, drawing blood. Dex muttered in concentration under his breath as the blood pooled in the circle.

I helped Chi into the center of the circle, both of us unsteady. I saw Monty reach the end of the bridge and drive the Sorrows into the ground. A keening wail began to fill the air. I saw Monty slam his hand on the ground and a blue wave of energy raced across the bridge.

The man on the bridge stopped and crouched. He threw up a shield as the wave washed over him. Monty pulled out the Sorrows and the bridge began to shudder as he raced back to where we were. Shockwaves rocked the bridge as it started to break apart.

Dropping the shield, the man took several steps toward us and then turned and ran in the opposite direction. The bridge disintegrated behind him until he reached the Jersey side. He turned to face us and formed another large orb of black energy.

"That looks incredibly painful." I pointed at the orb sailing our way. "Can we avoid the angry disintegration orb?"

Monty ran into the circle and looked at the blood. "A blood circle?" he whispered, looking at Dex. "You can't. The backlash will kill you, Uncle Dex."

"It's a risk." Dex nodded, pushing on the staff with a grunt. "If I don't, the lovely orb the magistrate is greeting us with will certainly do it."

Monty gestured and a series of orange runes settled over Dex. "Now." Monty looked up at the incoming orb of death. "Do it now!"

Dex placed his bloody hand on the staff. "Hold on to your knickers!" Dex yelled and slammed the staff the rest of the way into the ground. A green flash blinded me, and the island slipped away.

THE END

CAST OF CHARACTERS FOR BLOOD IS THICKER

ANDREI BELYAKOV-OLGA'S eyes and ears at The Moscow. He handles the day-to-day affairs of the building and reports to Olga. Has an instinctual self-preserving fear of Peaches.

Anastasia Anyxia Santiago-Leader of the Blood Hunters known as the most effective, zealous, and ruthless group to hunt down vampires.

Angel Ramirez-Director of the NYTF and friend to Simon Strong. Cannot believe how much destruction one detective agency can wage in the course of one day.

Claude-An accomplished mage and world-class assassin trained personally by Julien

Connor Montague-Father to Tristan and Elder of the Golden Circle.

Dex Montague-Uncle to Tristan, brother to Connor. One of the most powerful mages in the Golden Circle.

Erik Rothsfeld- Director of the Hellfire Club in NYC. Sitting Mage Representative on the Dark Council.

Estilete(Esti) Second in command to Anastasia Anyxia Santiago, leader of the Blood Hunters.

Gideon the Envoy-messengers sent to escort rogue mages back to the Sanctuary

The Hack-Cybercriminal, security expert, and friend of Simon. He is feared and hunted by every three-letter agency on the planet. If it's digital it's at risk.

Hades-Ruler of the Underworld. Rules the dead and is generally seen around funerals and wakes. Favorite song by the Eagles is 'Hotel California'-especially that part about checking out, but never leaving.

Ian Macintyre-Arbiter. Similar to Mage Police, which means they are some of the most powerful mages. When sent on a recovery, they are judge, jury, and executioner.

Julien Durant-Arch Mage of the Fleur de Lis. Owner and overseer of the Foundry-which exists as a de facto sovereign state within the city.

Ken Nakatomi-Michiko's brother and elite assassin for the Dark Council. If you're his target and you see him-it's the last thing you ever see.

Kali-(AKA Divine Mother) goddess of Time, Creation, Destruction, and Power. Cursed Simon for unspecified reasons and has been known to hold a grudge. She is also one of the most powerful magic-users in existence.

Karma-The personification of causality, order, and balance. She reaps what you sow. Also known as the mistress of bad timing. Everyone knows the saying karma is a…some days that saying is true.

Michiko Nakatomi-(AKA 'Chi' if you've grown tired of breathing) Vampire leader of the Dark Council. Reputed to be the most powerful vampire in the Council.

Noh Fan Yat- Martial arts instructor for the Montague & Strong Detective Agency. Teacher to both Simon and Tristan. Known for his bamboo staff of pain and correction.

Olga Etrechenko-Simon's landlord and current owner of The Moscow. She has an uncanny ability for tracking Simon down when the rent is due. You never cheat Olga.

Peaches-(AKA Devildog, Hellhound, Arm Shredder and Destroyer of Limbs) Offspring of Cerberus and given to the Montague & Strong Detective Agency to help with their security. Closely resembles a Cane Corso.

Piero Roselli-Vampire and owner of Roselli's-an upscale restaurant and club that caters to the supernatural community. If Piero doesn't seat you, you aren't staying.

Roxanne DeMarco-Director of Haven. Oversees both the Medical and Detention Centers of the facility. Is an accomplished sorceress with formidable skill. Has been known to make Tristan stammer and stutter with merely a touch of his arm.

Simon Strong-The intelligent (and dashingly handsome) half of the Montague & Strong Detective Agency. Cursed alive into immortality by the goddess Kali.

Tristan Montague- The civilized (and staggeringly brilliant) half of the Montague & Strong Detective Agency. Mage of the Golden Circle sect and currently on 'extended leave' from their ever-watchful supervision.

William Montague- Brother to Tristan Montague. Reported deceased-location unknown.

ORGANIZATIONS

CHRISTYE, BLAHQ, &DOIL-Law firm that shares the same floor with the Montague & Strong Detective Agency. Never seem to be open, but always ready for business.

New York Task Force-(AKA the NYTF) a quasi-military police force created to deal with any supernatural event occurring in New York City.

SuNaTran-(AKA Supernatural Transportations) Owned by Cecil Fairchild. Provides car and vehicle service to the supernatural community in addition to magic-users who can afford membership.

The Dark Council- Created to maintain the peace between humanity and the supernatural community shortly after the last Supernatural War. Its role is to be a check and balance against another war occurring. Not everyone in the Council favors peace.

AUTHOR NOTES

THANK YOU FOR reading this story and jumping back into the world of Monty & Strong. With each book, I want to introduce you to different elements of the world Monty & Strong inhabit, slowly revealing who they are and why they make the choices they do. If you want to know how they met, that story is in NO GOD IS SAFE, which is a short explaining how Tristan and Simon got started.

There are some references you may get and some… you may not. This may be attributable to my age (I'm older than Monty or feel that way most mornings) or to my love of all things sci-fi and fantasy. As a reader, I've always enjoyed finding these "Easter Eggs" in the books I read. I hope you do too. If there is a reference you don't get, feel free to email me and I will explain it…maybe.

You will notice that Simon is still a smart-ass (deserving a large head smack) and many times he's clueless about what's going on. Bear with him—he's still new to the immortal, magical world he's been delicately shoved into. Fortunately he has Monty to nudge (or blast) him in the right direction.

Each book will reveal more about Monty & Strong's backgrounds and lives before they met. Rather than hit you with a whole history, I wanted you to learn about them slowly, the way we do with a person we just met —over time (and many cups of coffee).

Thank you for taking the time to read this book. I wrote it for you and I hope you enjoyed spending a few more hours getting in (and out of) trouble with Tristan and Simon.

If you really enjoyed this story, I need you to do me a HUGE favor— **Please leave a review**.

It's really important and helps the book (and me). Plus, it means Peaches gets titanium chew toys, besides my arms, legs, and assorted furniture to shred.

We want to keep Peaches happy, don't we?

I really do appreciate your feedback. Let me know what you thought by emailing me at:
www.orlando@orlandoasanchez.com

For more information on Monty & Strong…come join the MoB on Facebook!

You can find us at:
Montague & Strong Case Files.

To get FREE books visit my page at:
www.orlandoasanchez.com

Still here? Amazing! Well, if you have made it this far —you deserve something special!

Included is the first chapter of the next Montague & Strong story-SILVER CLOUDS DIRTY SKY here for you to read.

Enjoy!

SILVER CLOUDS DIRTY SKY

SILVER CLOUDS DIRTY Sky
A Montague and Strong Book 4

Faith is the substance of things hoped for. The evidence of things not seen. -Hebrews 11:1

ONE

I hated teleportation.

We landed on smooth stone and I seriously considered never moving again. I looked up at the night sky. It took a few seconds before I realized we left New York City at dawn.

"Stay in the circle," Monty said and gestured. Light blue runes floated over us. "I can't determine the effects on a jump of that scale. It's safer if you stay inside."

"Where the hell are we, Monty?" I sat up and really looked around this time. Peaches was sprawled out, stunned, but moving slowly next to me. Beside him lay Michiko, unconscious. I didn't see Dex. I tried to stand

and the ground shifted in several directions, advising me that remaining seated was a good idea right now. "Where's Dex?"

Monty pointed with his chin while he kept gesturing. We were in a courtyard. A large squat stone building sat in front of us in the darkness. In fact, from what I could tell in the darkness, stone buildings surrounded us.

On the ground a few feet away lay Dex, with a woman next to him. It was hard to make out features, but the chill in the air gave me a clue.

"Monty," I whispered. "Is that—?"

She looked up at me then and I stared into the eyes of the Morrigan. Her eyes gave off a faint green glow as she laid Dex's head gently on the stone and approached.

"Which one of you allowed him to cast a spatial temporal circle—using his blood?" she asked with a smile.

That little voice I always ignored suggested burrowing into the stone and hiding. For once, I agreed with it.

"Well met, Morrigan," Monty said, stepping out of the circle and giving her a short bow.

"That remains to be seen, mage." She pointed at Dex without turning. "How did this happen?"

"He cast the blood circle to save us," Monty said, glancing back at the rest of us quickly. "No one tells my uncle what to do or when. You know that better than most. I did my best to limit the backlash. I didn't know he would be bringing us here or time-skipping."

"Where is *here*?" I asked, getting unsteadily to my

feet. The ground only wobbled slightly this time. In the dim light, I managed to make out a plaque affixed to the crumbling stone wall next to us which read: *Wardrobe Tower-12th Century.* "This isn't much of a wardrobe tower."

"The damn fool," Morrigan whispered and stepped back to Dex's body and knelt next to him. "He has exceeded his capacity and nearly killed himself in the process. What caused him to take such action?"

"We were evading a magistrate," Monty replied. "One sent to apprehend or eliminate me."

"That black orb that ate the Goat didn't say *apprehend* to me," I said, walking around the stone wall. Behind it stood a larger structure. "He was trying to kill us—especially you."

<*I'm hungry.*>

Peaches stirred and sniffed the air. I rubbed his belly as he stood on wobbly legs. Whatever we just did had hit him just as hard as it hit me. Michiko was still unconscious.

"I'll get you something to eat—as soon as I figure out where we are," I said, looking at Monty.

"The Consortium will be arriving soon," Morrigan said, scooping up Dex's body with little effort. A black raven swooped in and landed on her shoulder. "You will have to find another way to return. Your uncle will be in runic stasis for some time and the Consortium would like to have some words with him—violent words."

"He managed to anger them again, hasn't he?" Monty said with a shake of his head.

Morrigan smiled. "He's your uncle. Why ask

questions you can answer?"

"Consortium?" I looked at Monty. "There's no Consortium in New York."

The Penumbra Consortium was the older, darker, angrier, European version of the Dark Council—heavy hitters with long memories and longer reach. They oversaw and controlled the Western Hemisphere.

"You are correct, Simon." Morrigan flashed her green eyes at me and began phasing out of sight, taking Dex with her. "But then again, you are no longer in New York."

Her voice trailed off in the night as I turned to Monty. "Where did he teleport us?" I said, trying to keep my voice calm.

"It's more where and when." Monty adjusted his sleeves. "A blood circle allows the caster to incorporate an additional component to the teleportation circle—in this case it was a temporal component."

"Don't magicscience me—where and when the hell are we?"

"He took us to a place of power," Monty said, looking at the large stone structure in front of us. "*That* is the White Tower."

"White Tower as in Tower of London?" I asked incredulously. "He ported us to London?"

Monty nodded. "I would say a few hours ahead since we left New York City at dawn. London is five hours ahead and it's evening here. I could really use a cuppa."

"Why would he port us so far away?" I asked. "Even better, how did he do it?"

"I was just about to ask you the same thing," a voice behind me said. "Welcome to London. You are all under arrest."

Thank You!

If you enjoyed this book, would you please help me by leaving a review at the site where you purchased it from? It only needs to be a sentence or two and it would really help me out a lot!

All of My Books

The Warriors of the Way
The Karashihan* • Spiritual Warriors • The Ascendants • The Fallen Warrior • The Warrior Ascendant • The Master Warrior

John Kane
The Deepest Cut* • Blur

Sepia Blue
The Last Dance* • Rise of the Night

Chronicles of the Modern Mystics
The Dark Flame • A Dream of Ashes

Montague & Strong Detective Agency
Tombyards & Butterflies• Full Moon Howl•Blood Is Thicker•NoGod is Safe•The Date

*Books denoted with an asterisk are FREE via my website.
www.OrlandoASanchez.com

ACKNOWLEDGMENTS

I'm finally beginning to understand that each book, each creative expression usually has a large group of people behind it. This story is no different. So let me take a moment to acknowledge my (very large) group:

To Dolly: my wife and biggest fan. You make all of this possible and keep me grounded, especially when I get into my writing to the exclusion of everything else. Thank you, I love you.

To my Tribe: You are the reason I have stories to tell. You cannot possibly fathom how much and how deep I love you all.

To Lee: Because you were the first audience I ever had. I love you sis.

To the Logsdon family: JL your support always demands I bring my A-game and produce the best story I can. I always hear: "Don't rush!" in your voice.

LL (the Uber Jeditor) your notes and comments turned this story from good to great. I accept the challenge!

Your patience knows no bounds. Thank you both.

Arigatogozaimasu

The Montague & Strong Case Files Group AKA- The MoB(The Mages of BadAssery)

When I wrote T&B there were fifty-five members in The MoB. As of this writing there are 289 members in the MoB. I am honored to be able to call you my MoB Family. You are the reason I keep writing M&S and you help me make each story better. This is for all of you. I hope you enjoy it.

Thank you for being part of this group and M&S. You each make it possible.

THANK YOU.

To the ART Shredders

Thank you for taking of your time to read and shred this book. Each story is made better by your notes, observations, suggestions, and ideas.

Thank you so much for doing what you do. You have made this book fantastic.

YOU ARE AWESOME!!!

WTA-The Incorrigibles

JL, BenZ, EricQK, S.S., and the Mac

They sound like a bunch of badass misfits because they are. Thank you for making sure I didn't rush this one. My exposure to the slightly deranged and extremely deviant brain trust that you are made this book possible. I humbly thank you and…it's all your fault.

Special Mentions

Each book has a group of people that contribute in a special way.

Jim because my brain still melts when we speak lol.

Jen for the ancient post on old languages of the British Isles.

Sue because we magicscienced the hell out of this book.

Please forgive me if I missed a few (I always do).

The English Advisory(TEA)

Aaron, Penny, & Carrie

For all things English…thank you.

DEATH WISH COFFEE

Kane & Sierra for fueling the evenings(and

mornings) of frenzied activity with Odinforce & DeathWish blends.

Deranged Doctor Design

Kim, Darja, and Milo

You define professionalism and creativity. Thank you for the great service and amazing covers.

YOU GUYS RULE!

To you the reader:

Thank you for jumping down the rabbit hole with me. I truly hope you enjoy this story. You are the reason I wrote it.

ABOUT THE AUTHOR

Orlando Sanchez has been writing ever since his teens when he was immersed in creating scenarios for playing Dungeon and Dragons with his friends every weekend. An avid reader, his influences are too numerous to list here. Some of the most prominent are: J.R.R. Tolkien, Jim Butcher, Kat Richardson, Terry Pratchett, Christopher Moore,Terry Brooks, Piers Anthony, Lee Child, George Lucas, Andrew Vachss, and Barry Eisler to name a few in no particular order.

The worlds of his books are urban settings with a twist of the paranormal lurking just behind the scenes and generous doses of magic, martial arts, and mayhem.

Aside from writing, he holds a 2nd and 3rd Dan in two distinct styles of Karate. If not training, he is studying some aspect of the martial arts or martial arts philosophy.

He currently resides in Queens, NY with his wife and children and can often be found in the local Starbucks where most of his writing is done.

Please visit his site at OrlandoASanchez.com for more information about his books and upcoming releases.

This is a work of fiction. All of the characters, organizations, and events portrayed in this novel are either products of the author's imagination or are used fictitiously and are not to be construed as real. Any resemblance to actual events, locales, organizations, or persons, living or dead, is entirely coincidental.

Copyright © 2017 by Orlando A. Sanchez

All rights reserved, including the right to reproduce this book, or portions thereof, in any form.

Published by Bitten Peaches Publishing NY NY

Cover Design by Deranged Doctor Design
www.derangeddoctordesign.com